MORE VOICES FROM THE RADIUM AGE

The Radium Age Book Series
Joshua Glenn

Voices from the Radium Age, edited by Joshua Glenn, 2022
A World of Women, J. D. Beresford, 2022
The World Set Free, H. G. Wells, 2022
The Clockwork Man, E. V. Odle, 2022
Nordenholt's Million, J. J. Connington, 2022
Of One Blood, Pauline Hopkins, 2022
What Not, Rose Macaulay, 2022
The Lost World and The Poison Belt, Arthur Conan Doyle, 2023
Theodore Savage, Cicely Hamilton, 2023
The Napoleon of Notting Hill, G. K. Chesterton, 2023
The Night Land, William Hope Hodgson, 2023
More Voices from the Radium Age, edited by Joshua Glenn, 2023

MORE VOICES FROM THE RADIUM AGE

edited and introduced by
Joshua Glenn

THE MIT PRESS
CAMBRIDGE, MASSACHUSETTS
LONDON, ENGLAND

This book was set in Arnhem Pro and PF DIN Text Pro by New Best-set Typesetters Ltd. Printed and bound in the United States of America.

Library of Congress Cataloging-in-Publication Data

Names: Glenn, Joshua, 1967– editor, writer of introduction.
Title: More voices from the radium age / edited and introduced by Joshua Glenn.
Description: Cambridge, Massachusetts : The MIT Press, [2023] | Series: The Radium Age book series
Identifiers: LCCN 2022038603 (print) | LCCN 2022038604 (ebook) | ISBN 9780262546430 (paperback) | ISBN 9780262376082 (epub) | ISBN 9780262376075 (pdf)
Subjects: LCSH: Science fiction—20th century. | LCGFT: Short stories.
Classification: LCC PN6071.S33 M68 2023 (print) | LCC PN6071.S33 (ebook) | DDC 808.83/8762—dc23/eng/20221007
LC record available at https://lccn.loc.gov/2022038603
LC ebook record available at https://lccn.loc.gov/2022038604

10 9 8 7 6 5 4 3 2 1

CONTENTS

SERIES FOREWORD

Joshua Glenn

Do we really know science fiction? There were the scientific romance years that stretched from the mid-nineteenth century to circa 1900. And there was the genre's so-called golden age, from circa 1935 through the early 1960s. But between those periods, and overshadowed by them, was an era that has bequeathed us such tropes as the robot (berserk or benevolent), the tyrannical superman, the dystopia, the unfathomable extraterrestrial, the sinister telepath, and the eco-catastrophe. A dozen years ago, writing for the sf blog io9.com at the invitation of Annalee Newitz and Charlie Jane Anders, I became fascinated with the period during which the sf genre as we know it emerged. Inspired by the exactly contemporaneous career of Marie Curie, who shared a Nobel Prize for her discovery of radium in 1903, only to die of radiation-induced leukemia in 1934, I eventually dubbed this three-decade interregnum the "Radium Age."

Curie's development of the theory of radioactivity, which led to the extraordinary, terrifying, awe-inspiring insight that the atom is, at least in part, a state of energy constantly in movement, is an apt metaphor for the twentieth century's first three decades. These years were marked by rising sociocultural strife across various fronts: the founding of the women's suffrage movement, the National Association for the Advancement of Colored People, socialist currents within the labor movement, anticolonial and revolutionary upheaval around the world . . . as well as the associated strengthening of reactionary movements that supported, for example, racial segregation, immigration restriction, eugenics, and sexist policies.

Science—as a system of knowledge, a mode of experimenting, and a method of reasoning—accelerated the pace of change during these years in ways simultaneously liberating and terrifying. As sf author and historian Brian Stableford points out in his 1989 essay "The Plausibility of the Impossible," the universe we discovered by means of the scientific method in the early twentieth century defies common sense: "We are haunted by a sense of the impossibility of ultimately making sense of things." By playing host to certain far-out notions—time travel, faster-than-light travel, and ESP, for example—that we have every reason to judge impossible, science fiction serves as an "instrument of negotiation," Stableford suggests, with which we strive to accomplish "the difficult diplomacy of existence in a scientifically knowable but essentially unimaginable world." This is no less true today than during the Radium Age.

The social, cultural, political, and technological upheavals of the 1900–1935 period are reflected in the proto-sf writings of authors such as Olaf Stapledon, William Hope Hodgson, Muriel Jaeger, Karel Čapek, G. K. Chesterton, Cicely Hamilton, W. E. B. Du Bois, Yevgeny Zamyatin, E. V. Odle, Arthur Conan Doyle, Mikhail

Joshua Glenn

Bulgakov, Pauline Hopkins, Stanisław Ignacy Witkiewicz, Aldous Huxley, Gustave Le Rouge, A. Merritt, Rudyard Kipling, Rose Macaulay, J. D. Beresford, J. J. Connington, S. Fowler Wright, Jack London, Thea von Harbou, and Edgar Rice Burroughs, not to mention the late-period but still incredibly prolific H. G. Wells himself. More cynical than its Victorian precursor yet less hard-boiled than the sf that followed, in the writings of these visionaries we find acerbic social commentary, shock tactics, and also a sense of frustrated idealism—and reactionary cynicism, too—regarding humankind's trajectory.

The MIT Press's Radium Age series represents a much-needed evolution of my own efforts to champion the best proto-sf novels and stories from 1900 to 1935 among scholars already engaged in the fields of utopian and speculative fiction studies, as well as general readers interested in science, technology, history, and thrills and chills. By reissuing literary productions from a time period that hasn't received sufficient attention for its contribution to the emergence of science fiction as a recognizable form—one that exists and has meaning in relation to its own traditions and innovations, as well as within a broader ecosystem of literary genres, each of which, as John Rieder notes in *Science Fiction and the Mass Cultural Genre System* (2017), is itself a product of overlapping "communities of practice"—we hope not only to draw attention to key overlooked works but perhaps also to influence the way scholars and sf fans alike think about this crucial yet neglected and misunderstood moment in the emergence of the sf genre.

John W. Campbell and other Cold War–era sf editors and propagandists dubbed a select group of writers and story types from the pulp era to be the golden age of science fiction. In doing so, they helped fix in the popular imagination a too-narrow understanding of what the sf genre can offer. (In his introduction to the 1974 collection *Before the Golden Age*, for example, Isaac Asimov notes that although it may have possessed a certain exuberance, in general sf from before the mid-1930s moment when Campbell assumed editorship of *Astounding Stories* "seems, to anyone who has experienced the Campbell Revolution, to be clumsy, primitive, naive.") By returning to an international tradition of scientific speculation via fiction from after the Poe–Verne–Wells era and before sf's Golden Age, the Radium Age series will demonstrate— contra Asimov et al.—the breadth, richness, and diversity of the literary works that were responding to a vertiginous historical period, and how they helped innovate a nascent genre (which wouldn't be named until the mid-1920s, by Hugo Gernsback, founder of *Amazing Stories* and namesake of the Hugo Awards) as a mode of speculative imagining.

The MIT Press's Noah J. Springer and I are grateful to the sf writers and scholars who have agreed to serve as this series' advisory board. Aided by their guidance, we'll endeavor to surface a rich variety of texts, along with introductions by a diverse group of sf scholars, sf writers, and others that will situate these remarkable, entertaining, forgotten works within their own social, political, and scientific contexts, while drawing out contemporary parallels.

We hope that reading Radium Age writings, published in times as volatile as our own, will serve to remind us that our own era's seemingly natural, eternal, and inevitable social, economic, and cultural forms and norms are—like Madame Curie's atom—forever in flux.

INTRODUCTION: RADIUM AGE ULTRA-POTENTIALITIES

Joshua Glenn

During the early twentieth century, the world's scientists were wonderstruck by the revelation that the spontaneous disintegration of atoms (previously assumed to be indivisible and unchangeable) produces powerfully energetic "radio-active" emissions. Time, space, substance, our understanding of reality itself were called into question. "The man of science must have been sleepy indeed," as the author of *The Education of Henry Adams* would recall, "who did not jump from his chair like a scared dog when, in 1898, Mme. Curie threw on his desk the metaphysical bomb she called radium."

What Frederick Soddy, the English radiochemist whose lectures would inspire H. G. Wells to predict the atomic bomb, described as the "ultra-potentialities" of radioactive elements seemed limitless. Throughout the nineteen-aughts and -tens, scientists and snake-oil salesmen alike would ascribe to radium—and radiation in general—vitalizing, even life-giving powers. By the 1920s, then, the Soviet biochemist Alexander Oparin and the English biologist J. B. S. Haldane could independently propose that radiation, acting upon our planet's inorganic compounds billions of years ago, had produced a primordial "soup" from which emerged life.

Science fiction, too, emerged during the genre's 1900–1935 Radium Age from out of a hot dilute soup of sorts, this one composed of outré genres of literature—from occult mysteries and paranormal thrillers to Yukon adventures and Symbolist poetry—acted upon by the energy of new scientific and technological theories and breakthroughs. If a primary goal of the 2022 *Voices from the Radium Age* story collection was to showcase the proto-sf writings of authors whom few today would associate with the sf genre, this second collection offers instead an X-ray analysis of the diverse literary milieu out of which "science fiction" constructed itself.

George C. Wallis, author of the earliest story in this collection, first began writing scientific romances—a trilogy set in Atlantis, for example, as well as a riposte to Wells's *The War of the Worlds* in which Martians rescue Earth from meteors—during the late Victorian era. He'd continue writing sf right up into the genre's so-called Golden Age; his final novel would appear in 1948, a prolific half a century later.

Wallis's "The Last Days of Earth: Being the Story of the Launching of the 'Red Sphere'" (July 1901, in *The Harmsworth Magazine*) is another Wellsian yarn—this one reminiscent of *The Time Machine*. Some thirteen million years in the future we find Alwyn and Celia, humankind's designated survivors, channel-surfing between real-world scenes of frozen desolation. Sensitive readers may feel creeping into their bones an intimation of the decentering concept, first articulated by the geologist James

Hutton and more recently dubbed "Deep Time," that human civilization is fleetingly ephemeral in comparison with the literally glacial workings of nature.

Although there are futuristic gadgets here, from a worldwide Pictorial Telegraph relying on "reflected Marconi waves" to the titular planetary escape pod itself, this is no gung-ho tale of tech wizardry. Wallis's characters feel "the concentration and culmination of the woes and fears of the ages"; those of us aware, say, that the prospect of limiting global warming to 1.5 degrees Celsius may soon be out of reach can relate to the story's enervating atmosphere. Which is why the story's surprise twist, valorizing passion and "an heretical turn of mind," feels oddly hopeful.

Speaking of Wells, one of the prolific author's finest tales from this era predicts battle tanks—which wouldn't be deployed in the real world until the Battle of the Somme in 1916. "The Land Ironclads" (December 1903, in *The Strand*) depicts the defeat of a European country's military at the hands of a technologically advanced foe. It's the same plot as *The War of the Worlds*, really, only instead of Martians the invaders in armored fighting vehicles are fellow Europeans.

The correspondent through whose eyes we witness these events is conflicted. He deplores the "rowdy-dowdy" types who serve as his country's soldiery . . . yet when they are slaughtered by button-pushing clerks ("slender young men in blue pajamas," who may remind today's readers of drone jockeys fighting videogame-like telewars from the comfort of American suburbs), our man in the field inveighs against these "smart degenerates." Even as he spouts what Adorno would call the jargon of authenticity, however, he recognizes that war has become pointless.

Via subsequent Radium Age sf novels, including *The War in the Air*, which depicts German zeppelins devastating New York City, and *The World Set Free*, which hypothesizes the development of the most destructive weapon the world will ever see, Wells would urgently continue to make the case that there are—in the words of his correspondent—"other things in life better worth having than proficiency in war."

"The Republic of the Southern Cross," which appeared in Valery Bryusov's 1907 collection *Zemnaya Os* (*Earth's Axis*), and which was translated into English in 1918, is an account of the fate of Zvezdny (Star City), domed capital of a workers' utopia situated atop the South Pole.

A decade before Yevgeny Zamyatin's dystopian *We*, which explores similar themes, Bryusov asks us to imagine a society in which efficiency has been extended into all spheres of life. The city's temperature and light are regulated, and "the life of the citizens was standardized even to the most minute details." Small wonder, then, that a "psychical distemper" should influence the city's residents to do the opposite of whatever is efficient and reasonable. Hilarity, which soon gives way to gruesomely depicted carnage, ensues.

Like other Symbolist poets who dabbled in proto-sf writing, Bryusov, a leader of the Russian Symbolist movement, was fascinated with the notion that "the days shall come of final desolation"—to quote one of his poems. "We are weary of conventional forms of society, conventional forms of morality, the very means of perception, everything that comes from outside," he'd announced in 1903. "It is becoming clearer and clearer that if what we see is all that there is in the world, then there is nothing worth living for." This could serve as a fitting epitaph for Star City.

E. Nesbit, the English author known today for *Five Children and It* and other wry, intelligent contemporary fantasies that paved the way for future fantasists from C. S. Lewis to J. K. Rowling, was a friend of H. G. Wells and a prolific writer of horror stories, some of them sf-inflected. Published under her frequent pseudonym E. Bland, Nesbit's "The Third Drug" (February 1908, in *The Strand*) is an early example of proto-sf horror.

Body-snatched and confined by a mad scientist, our protagonist, Roger, is injected with two drugs. It is via the third drug, the scientist claims, "that life—splendid, superhuman life—is found." Indeed, upon receiving his booster shot Roger does appear to develop unnatural strength, not to mention a sensation of omniscience. Predating J. D. Beresford's *The Hampdenshire Wonder* by a year, and other intelligence-oriented superman stories (John Taine's *Seeds of Life*, say, or Olaf Stapledon's *Last Men in London*) by over two decades, this is literally heady stuff.

It's worth noting that Roger isn't much less scornful of his fellow man than is his kidnapper: During the struggle with Parisian apaches that precedes his capture, he is disgusted by their "pale, degenerate" faces and their subhuman odor. In the end, however, he discovers that "the old common sense that guides an ordinary man" trumps even a superman's "consciousness of illimitable wisdom" . . . and that humanity inheres within even a hooligan's heart.

If Bryusov wished to revolutionize our means of perception, then "A Victim of Higher Space" (December 1914, in *The Occult Review*), by the English "weird fiction" pioneer Algernon Blackwood, warns those of us who share this goal to be wary. In this sequel to the author's 1908 collection of stories about occult detective John Silence, a psychonaut named Mudge who has been meditating upon a four-dimensional cube diagram seeks Silence's counsel—because he has slipped into a space-time of infinite dimensions!

The John Silence stories sit at the nexus of what sf historian Paul March-Russell has described as this era's "mesh of mathematics and mysticism." Like other weird fiction authors, Blackwood was a member of the Hermetic Order of the Golden Dawn, a society devoted to the semi-scientific study and practices of the occult, metaphysics, and the paranormal. Paranormal researchers of the era were enthralled by theories of higher-dimensional spaces which, since the 1880s, had been promulgated by the eminent mathematician Charles Howard Hinton—who urged dimension-curious seekers to develop their intuitive perception of hyperspace.

Blackwood's stories offer us a visceral sense of the appeal of a research methodology that can marry the thrill of scientific discovery with the irrational awe vouchsafed by a vision (like poor Mudge's) of "a monstrous world, so utterly different to all we know and see that I cannot even hint at the nature of the sights and objects and beings in it."

One of the most popular authors of weird fiction in the United States—"different stories," per pulp magazine editors at the time—was Abraham Merritt, who wrote as A. Merritt. His sf-inflected novels of the era, including *The Moon Pool* (1918) and *The Face in the Abyss* (1923), suggested that alien races and ancient technologies were to be discovered beneath the surface of everyday life—literally beneath the surface, as the explorer Stanton discovers, to his horror, in "The People of the Pit" (January 5, 1918, in *All-Story Weekly*).

Stanton recounts his sojourn in an underground Alaskan city inhabited by fiends "like the ghosts of inconceivably monstrous slugs." A canyon is so deep, we read, that it's "like peeping over the edge of a cleft world down into the infinity where the planets roll!" Describing altar-carvings, Stanton insists that "the human eye cannot grasp them any more than it can grasp the shapes that haunt the fourth dimension." If this language reminds you of H. P. Lovecraft's, the story was in fact a key influence on *At the Mountains of Madness* and other Lovecraft efforts.

By today's standards, as the Golden Age sf author Jack Williamson, who got his start during the Radium Age, would recall years later, "the kind of style Merritt was creating seems excessive, florid and adjective-laden." However, as Williamson goes on to insist, Merritt's proto-sf stories—which hinted at cosmic horror beyond our ken—will reward today's sf readers' attention, thanks to their "emphasis on color, wonder, the magic of sheer imagination."

In George Allan England's "The Thing from—'Outside'," a creature that may hail not merely from off-world but from a dimension "outside the universe" stalks an expedition in the Canadian wilderness. A science-fictional updating of Blackwood's 1910 horror tale "The Wendigo," the story appeared in the April 1923 issue of Hugo Gernsback's magazine *Science and Invention*.

England, a popular American pulp fiction writer best known for his (racist) Darkness and Dawn trilogy, creates here an atmosphere of stifling paranoia. Jandron, a geologist, feels a "gnawing at the base of his brain"; members of the expedition begin to perceive reality as though through a glass darkly; they quarrel and turn on one another. All of which may remind John Carpenter fans of *The Thing*. Which would make perfect sense, since Carpenter's 1982 movie, set in Antarctica, is an adaptation of Golden Age sf writer and editor John W. Campbell's 1938 story "Who Goes There?"—which was influenced by "The Thing from—'Outside'."

At one point, Jandron name-checks Charles Fort, the eccentric American researcher and author who in works like 1919's *The Book of the Damned* presented readers with anomalous phenomena, criticized scientific dogmatism, and proposed (semi-humorous) theories about alien astronauts and the like. "If you knew more," Jandron chastises his companions, whose refusal to consider Fortean theories he considers narrow-minded, "you'd know a devilish sight less." This pronunciamento could be a slogan for the many proto-sf stories influenced by Fort's writings.

A modernist poet, novelist, and critic who published as May Sinclair, Mary Amelia St. Clair is best remembered for semi-autobiographical novels such as 1922's *Life and Death of Harriett Frean*. However, she also published supernatural and proto-sf fiction in which mysticism, spirituality, psychoanalysis, and idealist philosophy were intermingled.

Playfully exploring the metaphysical and moral implications of Einstein's Special Theory of Relativity, as well as the hyperspatial theories of scientists and psychical researchers, Sinclair's "The Finding of the Absolute" (1923, in the author's collection *Uncanny Stories*) follows the afterlife adventures of Mr. Spalding, a narrow-minded Kantian philosopher who is shocked to discover that his adulterous wife and her lover have been granted entrance to Heaven. But his 3D worldview and value system, the spirit of Kant himself explains to him, is inadequate . . . because the universe operates on the rules of four-dimensional reality.

One of the first critics to use the phrase "stream of consciousness" in a literary context, Sinclair takes us on a joy-ride through "an unseen web, intensely vibrating, stretched through all space and all time." The ecstatic flip side of Mr. Mudge's nightmare, Mr. Spalding's vision is of a multidimensional reality "utterly plastic to our imagination and our will." Small wonder that T. S. Eliot and Jorge Luis Borges would sing the praises of the still-underappreciated Sinclair.

Our final story is the sole sf effort by an author who twice won the Pulitzer Prize for fiction; in fact, during his lifetime Booth Tarkington was considered America's greatest living author. If he is mostly forgotten today, it is because—like the reactionary protagonist of his 1918 novel *The Magnificent Ambersons*—he was fixated on the negative consequences of progress, which may help us puzzle out the meaning of "The Veiled Feminists of Atlantis" (March 1926, in *Forum*).

Written not long after the 19th Amendment guaranteed American women the right to vote, Tarkington's satire reimagines the legend of Atlantis's demise as a war between the sexes. Having agitated for the opportunity to learn the menfolk's "magic"—which is to say, technology sufficiently advanced to be indistinguishable from magic—the women of Atlantis achieve not only social, economic, and political equality but predominance . . . at which point they willingly re-adopt the veils that, during their campaign for equality, they'd cast off. Outraged at their own loss of status and power (much like today's white nationalists), Atlantis's menfolk revolt.

The sf historian Sam Moskowitz would anthologize Tarkington's story in a 1972 collection, *When Women*

Joshua Glenn

Rule—thus suggesting that it predicts and celebrates women's liberation. Writing in a 1980 issue of *Science Fiction Studies*, though, New Wave sf author Joanna Russ would disagree. "One discerns the familiar charges," she writes: "that the rule of women over men is unjust (but the rule of men over women was benevolent), and that women's use of power will be immoral and destructive." Readers can make up their own minds.

Tarkington's fable, as well as the other proto-sf stories collected here and in the first *Voices of the Radium Age* collection (not to mention the novels reissued via MIT Press's Radium Age series), can spark lively intellectual debate . . . and send us on mind-bending voyages into the dimension of imagination. So be careful! The book you're holding practically vibrates with unknown energies and spine-tingling ultra-potentialities.

THE LAST DAYS OF EARTH
BEING THE STORY OF THE LAUNCHING OF THE 'RED SPHERE'

George C. Wallis

A man and a woman sat facing each other across a table in a large room. They were talking slowly, and eating— eating their last meal on earth. The end was near; the sun had ceased to warm, was but a red-hot cinder outwardly; and these two, to the best of their belief, were the last people left alive in a world-wilderness of ice and snow and unbearable cold.

The woman was beautiful—very fair and slight, but with the tinge of health upon her delicate skin and the fire of intellect in her eyes. The man was of medium height, broad-shouldered, with wide, bald head and resolute mien—a man of courage, dauntless purpose, strenuous life. Both were dressed in long robes of a thick, black material, held in at the waist by a girdle.

As they talked, their fingers were busy with a row of small white knobs let into the surface of the table, and marked with various signs. At the pressure of each knob a flap in the middle of the table opened, and a small glass vessel, with a dark, semi-liquid compound steaming in it, was pushed up. As these came, in obedience to the tapping of their fingers, the two ate their contents with the aid of tiny spoons. There was no other dining apparatus or dinner furniture upon the table, which stood upon a single but massive pedestal of grey metal.

The meal over, the glasses and spoons replaced, the table surface clean and clear, a silence fell between them. The man rested his elbows upon his knees and his chin upon his upturned palms. He did not look at his fair companion, but beyond her, at a complicated structure projecting from the wall. This was the Time Indicator, and gave, on its various discs, the year, the month, the day, the hour and the instant, all corrected to mean astronomical time and to the exact latitude and longitude of the place. He read the well-known symbols with defiant eyes. He saw that it was just a quarter to thirteen in the afternoon of Thursday, July 18th, 13,000,085 A.D. He reflected that the long association of the place with time-recording had been labour spent in vain. The room was in a great building on the site of ancient Greenwich. In fact, the last name given to the locality by its now dead and cold inhabitants had been Grenijia.

From the time machine, the man's gaze went round the room. He noted, with apparently keen interest, all the things that were so familiar to him—the severely plain walls, transparent on one side, but without window-frame or visible door in their continuity; the chilling prospect of a faintly-lit expanse of snow outside; the big telescope that moved in an airtight slide across the ceiling, and the little motor that controlled its motions; the electric radiators that heated the place, forming an almost unbroken dado round the walls; the globe of pale brilliance that hung in the middle of the room and assisted the twilight glimmer of the day; the neat library of books and photo-phono cylinders, and the tier of speaking machines

George C. Wallis

beneath it; the bed in the further corner, surrounded by yet more radiators; the two ventilating valves; the great dull disc of the Pictorial Telegraph: and the thermometer let into a vacant space of floor. On this last his glance rested for some time, and the woman's also. It registered the degrees from absolute zero; and stood at a figure equivalent to 42° Fahrenheit. From this tell-tale instrument the eyes of the two turned to each other, a common knowledge shining in each face. The man was the first to speak again.

"A whole degree, Celia, since yesterday. And the dynamos are giving out a current at a pressure of 6,000 volts. I can't run them at any higher efficiency. That means that any further fall of temperature will close the drama of this planet. Shall we go tonight?"

There was no quiver of fear nor hint of resentment in his voice, nor in the voice that answered him. Long ages of mental evolution had weeded all the petty vices and unreasoning passions out of the mind of man.

"I am ready any time, Alwyn. I do not like to go; I do not like the risk of going; but it is our last duty to the humanity behind us—and I must be with you to the end."

There was another silence between them; a silence in which the humming of the dynamos in the room below seemed to pervade the whole place, thrilling through everything with annoying audibility. Suddenly the man leaned forward, regarding his companion with a puzzled expression.

"Your eyelashes are damp, Celia. You are not crying? That is too archaic."

"I must plead guilty," she said, banishing the sad look with an effort. "We are not yet so thoroughly adjusted to our surroundings as to be able to crush down every weak impulse. Wasn't it the day before yesterday that you said the sun had begun to cool about five million years too soon for man? But I will not give way again. Shall we start at once?"

"That is better; that sounds like Celia. Yes, if you wish, at once; but I had thought of taking a last look round the world—at least, as far as the telegraph system is in order. We have three hours' daylight yet."

For answer, Celia came and sat beside him on the couch facing the disc of the Pictorial Telegraph. His left hand clasped her right; both were cold. With his right hand he pulled over and held down a small lever under the disc—one of many, each bearing a distinctive name and numeral.

The side wall became opaque; the globe ceased to be luminous. A moving scene grew out of the dullness of the disc, and a low, moaning sound stole into the room. They looked upon a telegraphically-transmitted view of a place near which had once been Santiago, Chile. There were the ruins of an immense white city there now, high on the left of the picture. Down on the right, far below the well-defined marks of six successive beach-lines, a cold sea moaned over an icy bar, and dashed in semi-frozen spray under the bluff of an overhanging glacier's edge.

Out to sea great bergs drifted slowly, and the distant horizon was pale with the ice-blink from vast floes. The view had scarcely lasted a moment, when a great crack appeared on the top of the ice-front, and a huge fragment fell forward into the sea. It overturned on the bar, churning up a chaos of foam, and began to drift away. At the same instant came the deafening report of the breakage. There was no sign of life, neither of man nor beast, nor bird nor fish, in that cold scene. Polar bears and Arctic foxes, blubber-eating savages and hardy seals, had all long since passed away, even from the tropic zone.

Another lever pressed down, and the Rock of Gibraltar appeared on the disc. It rose vast and grim from the ice-arched waters of a shallow strait, with a vista of plain and mountain and glacier stretching behind it to the hazy distance—a vista of such an intolerable whiteness that the two watchers put on green spectacles to look at it. On the flat top of the Rock—which ages ago had been levelled to make it an alighting station for the Continental aerial machines—rose, gaunt and frost-encrusted, the huge skeleton framework of one of the last flying conveyances used by man.

Another lever, and Colombo, Ceylon, glared lifeless on the disc. Another, and Nagasaki, Japan, the terminal front of a vast glacier, frowned out over a black, ice-filling sea. Yet more levers, and yet more scenes; and everywhere ice and snow, and shallow, slowly-freezing seas; or countries here black and plantless, and there covered with glaciers from the crumbling hills. No sign of life, save the vestiges of man's now-ended reign, and of his long fight with the relentless cold—here ruins, on the ice-free levels, of his Cities of Heat; here gigantic moats, excavated to retard the glaciers; here canals, to connect the warmer seas;

here the skeletons of huge metallic floating palaces jetti-
soned on some ice-bound coast; and everywhere that the
ice had not overcome, the tall masts of the Pictorial Telegraph, sending to the watchers at Greenwich, by reflected
Marconi waves, a presentment of each sight and sound
impinging on the speculums and drums at their summits.
And in every daylight scene, the pale ghost of a dim, red
sun hung in a clear sky.

In the more northern and southern views the magnetic
lights were as brilliant as ever, but there were no views of
the extreme Polar Regions. These were more inaccessible
than in the remote past, for there cakes and patches of
liquid and semi-solid air were slowly settling and spread-
ing on land and sea.

Yet more levers, and yet more; and the two turned away
from the disc; and the room grew light again.

"It appears just as we have seen it these last two years,"
said the man, "yet to-day the tragedy of it appalls me as it
has never done before. I did not think, after all the years
of expectation and mental schooling, that it would seem
like this at the last I feel tempted to do as our parents
did—to seek the safety of the Ultimate Silence."

"Not that, Alwyn—not that. From generation to generation this day has been foreseen and prepared for, and we
promised, after we were chosen to remain, that we would
not die until all the devices of our science failed. Let us go
down and get ready to leave at once."

Celia's face had a glow upon it, a glow that Alwyn's
caught.

"I only said 'tempted,' Celia. Were I alone, I do not think I should break my word. And I am also curious. And the old, strange desire for life has come to me. And you are here. Let me kiss you, Celia. That . . . at least, is not archaic."

They walked hand-in-hand to a square space marked out on the floor in a corner of the room, and one of them pressed a button on the wall. The square sank with them, lowering them into a dimmer room, where the ceaseless humming of the dynamos became a throbbing roar. They saw, with eyes long used to faint light, the four great alternators spinning round the armatures; felt the fanning of the rapid revolutions upon their faces. By the side of each machine they saw the large, queer-shaped chemical engines that drove them, that were fed from dripping vats, and from many actions and reactions supplied the power that stood between their owners and the cold that meant the end. Coal had long been exhausted, along with peat and wood and all inflammable oils and gases; no turbines could be worked from frozen streams and seas; no air wheels would revolve in an atmosphere but slightly stirred by a faded sun. The power in chemical actions and reactions, in transmutations and compoundings of the elements, was the last great source of power left to man in the latter days.

After a brief glance round the room, they pressed another button, and the lift went down to a still lower floor. Here a small glow-lamp was turned on, and they stood before a sphere of bright red metal that filled the greater part of the room. They had not seen this many times in their lives. Its meaning was too forcible a reminder of a prevision for the time that had at last arrived.

The Red Sphere was made of a manufactured element, unknown except within the last million years, and so costly and troublesome to produce that only two Red Spheres had ever been built. It had been made 500 years before Alwyn and Celia were born. It was made for the purpose of affording the chosen survivors of humanity a means of escaping from the earth when the chemical power proved incapable of resisting the increasing cold. In the Red Sphere Alwyn and Celia intended to leave the earth, to plunge into space—not to seek warmth and light on any other member of the Solar System, for that would be useless—but to gain the neighbourhood of some yet young and fiery star. It was a terrible undertaking—as much more terrible than mere interplanetary voyages as the attempt of a savage to cross the Atlantic in his dugout after having learned to navigate his own narrow creek. It had been left undared until the last, when, however slight the chance of life in it, the earth could only offer instead the choice of soon and certain death.

"It appears just as it did the day I first saw it and was told its purpose," said Celia, with a shudder she could not repress. "Are you sure, Alwyn, that it will carry us safely?—that you can follow out the Instructions?"

For generations the Red Sphere and all appertaining to it had been mentioned with a certain degree of awe.

"Don't trouble yourself on that point. The Instructions are simple. The necessary apparatus, and the ten years' supply of imperishable nutriment, are already inside and fixed. We have only to subject the Red Metal to our 6,000 volt current for an hour, get inside, screw up the inlet, and cut ourselves adrift. The Red Metal, thus electrified, becomes, as you know, repulsive to gravitation, and will so continue for a year and a half. By that time, as we shall travel, according to calculation, at twice the speed of light, we should be more than half-way to one of the nearer stars, and so become subject to its gravitation. With the earth in its present position, if we start in a couple of hours, we should make F. 188, mag. 2, of the third order of spectra. Our sun, according to the records, belonged to the same order. And we know that it has at least two planets."

"But if we fall right into F. 188, instead of just missing it, as we hope? Or if we miss, but so closely as to be fused by its heat? Or if we miss it too widely and are thrown back into space on a parabolic or hyperbolic orbit? Or if we should manage the happy medium and find there be no life, nor any chance of life, upon the planets of that system? Or if there be life, but it be hostile to us?"

"Those are the inevitable dangers of our plunge, Celia. The balance of probabilities is in favour of either the first or second of those things befalling us. But that is not the same as absolute certainty, and the improbable *may* happen."

"Quite so, Alwyn; but—do you recollect if the Instructions make any reference to these possibilities?"

"To—? Yes. There is enough fulminate of sterarium packed in the Sphere to shiver it and us to fine dust in the thousandth part of a second—if we wish. We shall always have that resource. Now I'll attach the dynamo leads to the Sphere. Get your little items of personal property together, and we shall be ready."

Celia went up the lift again, and Alwyn, after fixing the connections to several small switches on the surface of the Sphere, followed her. They sat together in the darkening twilight of the dim room above, waiting for the first hour to pass. They spoke at intervals, and in fragmentary phrases.

"It will be cold while the Sphere is being prepared," said Alwyn.

"Yes, but we shall be together, dear, as we have been so long now. I remember how miserable I felt when I first knew my destiny; but when I learned that you were chosen to share it with me, I was glad. But you were not, Alwyn—you loved Amy?"

"Yes."

"And you love her still, but you love me, too? Do you know why she was not chosen?"

"Yes; I love you, Celia, though not so much as I loved Amy. They chose you instead of her, they said, because you had a stronger will and greater physical vigour. The slight curve we shall describe on rising will bring us over the Heat-house she and her other lover retired to after the Decision, and we shall perhaps see whether they are really dead, as we believe. Amy, I remember, had an heretical turn of mind."

"If they are not dead, it is strange that they should not have answered our Marconi and telepathic messages after the first year—unless, of course, as you have so often suggested, they have retired to the interior of the other Red Sphere. How strange that it should have been left there! If they have only enough food, they may live in it till old age intervenes, secure from all the rigours that approach, but what a tame end—what a prisonment!"

"Terrible. I could not endure the Red Sphere except as we shall endure it—travelling."

So the hour passed. They switched the electric current into the framework of the vehicle that was to bear them into space. All the radiators ceased to glow and all the lights went out, leaving them, in that lower room, in absolute darkness and intense cold. They sat huddled together against the wall, where they could feel the thrill of the humming dynamos, embracing each other, silent and resolute; waiting for the end of the cold hour. They could find few words to speak now, but their thoughts were the busier.

They thought of the glorious, yet now futile past, with all its promises shattered, its ideals valueless, its hopes unfulfilled; and seemed to feel in themselves the concentration and culmination of the woes and fears of the ages. They saw, as in one long vista, the history of the millions of vanished years—"from earth's nebulous origin to its final ruin"; from its days of four hours to its days of twenty-six and a half; from its germinating specks of primal protoplasm to its last and greatest, and yet most evil creature, Man. They saw, in mental perspective, the uneven periods of human progress; the long stages of advance and retrogression, of failure and success. They saw the whole long struggle between the tendencies of Egoism and Altruism, and knew how these had merged at last into an automatic equilibration of Duty and Desire. They saw the climax of this equilibration, the Millennium of Man—and they knew how the inevitable decay had followed.

They saw how the knowledge of the sureness and nature of life's end had come to Man; slowly at first, and not influencing him much, but gaining ever more and more power as the time grew nearer and sympathy and intellect more far-sighted and acute; how, when the cold itself began, and the temperate zone grew frigid, and the tropic temperate, and Man was compelled to migrate, and his sources of heat and power failed one after the other, the knowledge of the end reacted on all forms of mental activity, throwing all thought and invention into one groove. They saw the whole course of the long fight; the ebb and flow of the struggle against the cold, in which, after each long period, it was seen that Man was the loser; how men, armed with powers that to their ancestors would have made them seem as gods, had migrated to the other planets of the system, only to find that there, even on Mercury himself, the dying sun had made all life a fore-known lost battle; how many men, whole nations, had sought a premature refuge from the Fear in the Ultimate Silence called Death. They saw how all the old beliefs, down to the tiniest shreds of mysticism, had fallen from Man as a worn-out garment, leaving him spiritually naked to face the terrors of a relentless Cosmos: how, in the slow dissolving of the ideal Future, man's duties and thoughts were once more moulded with awe and reverence to the wishes of the Past.

They saw the closing centuries of the struggle; the discovery of the Red Metal; the building of the Spheres that none dare venture to use, but which each succeeding and lessening generation handed down to the next as a sacred heritage only to be put to test in the last resort; they remembered, in their own childhood, the Conference of the Decision, when they two had been chosen, as the only pair of sufficient vigour and health and animal courage to accept the dread legacy and dare the dread adventure of seeking a fresh home in the outer vastness, so that haply the days of Man might not be ended; and they remembered, only too well, how the rest of humanity, retiring to their last few houses, had one and all pledged each other to seek the Silence and trouble the chilly earth no more. They knew how well that pledge had been kept, and in the darkness and silence of the room clutched each other closer and closer.

And at last they heard the Time Indicator in the uppermost room ring the peal of the completed hour, and knew that in their own lives they must act the final scene in the long life-tragedy of the earth.

Alwyn's hand reached out and touched the switch, and the glow-lamp sprang into radiance again. In silence he handed Celia into the Sphere—which shone a deeper red now and coruscated strangely in the light—and then followed her, drawing the screw section in after him and making it secure. Within, the Sphere was spacious and comfortable, and, save where thickly padded, transparent, even to the weak incandescence of the lamp. It was also pleasantly warm, for the Red Metal was impervious to heat. The man's hand went to the lever that worked through the shell, and pushed aside the strong jaws of the spring clamp that held the Sphere down; and as it went, he looked into the woman's eyes. He hesitated. There was a light in her eyes and his, a feeling in her heart and his, that neither had seen nor experienced before.

"It's madness, Celia," he said, slowly. "It's not too late yet. The moment I pull this lever over the Sphere will tear its way up through the building like an air-bubble through water, but until then it is not too late."

This was not a question in phrase, but it was in fact. Celia did not answer.

"Isn't it a miserable folly—this deference to the past? Don't we know perfectly well that death is as certain out there as here?" the man went on.

Then Celia answered: "Yes, Alwyn; Man, life, everything, is a most miserable folly. But we have nothing to do with that; we can't help it. We don't know, until we try, what fortune may yet meet us. We should be untrue to our ancestors, cowards and recreants to ourselves, if we drew back now. Even in face of the unconscious enmity of the whole Universe of Matter, let us remember that we are living and conscious yet."

As so often in the past, the woman was the man's strengthener in the time of need. Alwyn pulled over the lever, and cried, with antique impulsiveness:—

"Forgive me, Celia! We will not give in, not even against a hostile universe! She moves!—we go!"

There was a sudden shock that threw them staggering against each other for a moment; a rending, tearing, rolling crash of masonry and metal, and the Red Sphere rose through the falling ruins of the house and soared up into the night, slanting slightly to the west as it rose. One brief glimpse they had of the dials of the Time Indicator falling across a gap of the ruin; and then their eyes were busy with the white face of earth beneath and the clear brilliance of the starry dome above.

They were still clinging to each other, when both caught sight of a small dark object approaching them from beneath. It came, apparently, from a black spot on the chill whiteness of the landscape to the west of their abandoned home, and it was travelling faster than themselves.

They gazed down at it with sudden interest, that, as they gazed, turned into acute apprehension, and then to a numb horror.

"The other Sphere!"

"Amy and her lover!"

While they spoke it grew definitely larger, and they saw that a collision was unavoidable. By what caprice of fate it had so fallen out that the helpless paths of the two Red Spheres should thus come to coincide in a point of space and time, they could not imagine. The idea of leaving the earth might, by magnetic sympathy, have occurred to both couples at about the same time, but the rest of the unlucky coincidence was inexplicable. They turned from looking at the second Sphere and sought each other's eyes and hands, saying much by look and pressure that words could not convey.

"They did not mean to keep the pledge of the Decision," said Alwyn. "The desire for life must have come to them as it came to me to-day, and Amy must have remembered the Instructions. I can understand them coming up faster than us, because their Sphere was in a sheet-metal shed in the open, and so would start with less opposition and greater initial velocity. But it is strange that their path should be so nearly ours. It can only be a matter of minutes, at the rate they are gaining, before the end comes for all of us. It will be before we get through the atmosphere and gather our full speed. And it will be the end of Humanity's troubled dream . . . And Amy is in that . . ."

The thought of possible malice, impulsive or premeditated, on the part of the occupants of the second Red Sphere, never entered into the minds of those of the first.

"The responsibility of action rests upon us," said Celia. "They evidently cannot see us, against the background of the black sky. They are coming up swiftly, dear."

"It will have to be that: there is no other way. Better one than both," said the man.

"Be what, Alwyn?"

"The fulminate of sterarium."

"It will not injure them?"

"No; not if we fire the fuse within—about—three minutes. It must seem hard to you, Celia, to know that my hand will send you to the Silence so that Amy may have the last desperate chance of life. Somehow, these last few hours, I have felt the ancient emotions surging back."

The hand that clasped his gave a gentle pressure.

George C. Wallis

"And I, too, Alwyn; but their reign will be brief. I would rather die with you now than live without you. I am ready. Do not be too late with the fulminate, Alwyn."

They swayed together; their arms were about each other; their lips met in the last kiss. While their faces were yet very near, Alwyn's disengaged right hand touched a tiny white button that was embedded in the padding of the interior.

There was an instantaneous flash of light and roar of sound, and the man and woman in the second sphere were startled by the sudden glare and concussion of it, as their metal shell drove upwards through the cloud of elemental dust that was all that remained of the first Red Sphere and its occupants.

The silence and clear darkness that had been round them a moment before, had returned when they recovered their balance; and in that silence and clear darkness, the man and woman who had not been chosen passed out into the abyss of the Beyond, ignorant of the cause and meaning of that strange explosion in the air, and knew that they were alone in Space, bound they knew not whither.

1901

THE LAND IRONCLADS

H. G. Wells

I.

The young lieutenant lay beside the war correspondent and admired the idyllic calm of the enemy's lines through his field-glass.

"So far as I can see," he said, at last, "one man."

"What's he doing?" asked the war correspondent.

"Field-glass at us," said the young lieutenant.

"And this is war!"

"No," said the young lieutenant, "it's Bloch."

"The game's a draw."

"No! They've got to win or else they lose. A draw's a win for our side."

They had discussed the political situation fifty times or so, and the war correspondent was weary of it. He stretched out his limbs. "Aaai s'pose it *is*!" he yawned.

"*Flut!*"

"What was that?"

"Shot at us."

The war correspondent shifted to a slightly lower position. "No one shot at him," he complained.

"I wonder if they think we shall get so bored we shall go home?"

The war correspondent made no reply.

"There's the harvest, of course. . . ."

They had been there a month. Since the first brisk movements after the declaration of war things had gone slower and slower, until it seemed as though the whole machine of events must have run down. To begin with, they had had almost a scampering time; the invader had come across the frontier on the very dawn of the war in half-a-dozen parallel columns behind a cloud of cyclists and cavalry, with a general air of coming straight on the capital, and the defender horsemen had held him up, and peppered him and forced him to open out to outflank, and had then bolted to the next position in the most approved style, for a couple of days, until in the afternoon, bump! they had the invader against their prepared lines of defense. He did not suffer so much as had been hoped and expected: he was coming on, it seemed with his eyes open, his scouts winded the guns, and down he sat at once without the shadow of an attack and began grubbing trenches for himself, as though he meant to sit down there to the very end of time. He was slow, but much more wary than the world had been led to expect, and he kept convoys tucked in and shielded his slow marching infantry sufficiently well to prevent any heavy adverse scoring.

"But he ought to attack," the young lieutenant had insisted.

"He'll attack us at dawn, somewhere along the lines. You'll get the bayonets coming into the trenches just about when you can see," the war correspondent had held until a week ago.

The young lieutenant winked when he said that.

H. G. Wells

When one early morning the men the defenders sent to lie out five hundred yards before the trenches, with a view to the unexpected emptying of magazines into any night attack, gave way to causeless panic and blazed away at nothing for ten minutes, the war correspondent understood the meaning of that wink.

"What would you do if you were the enemy?" said the war correspondent, suddenly.

"If I had men like I've got now?"

"Yes."

"Take those trenches."

"How?"

"Oh—dodges! Crawl out half-way at night before moonrise and get into touch with the chaps we send out. Blaze at 'em if they tried to shift, and so bag some of 'em in the daylight. Learn that patch of ground by heart, lie all day in squatty holes, and come on nearer next night. There's a bit over there, lumpy ground, where they could get across to rushing distance—easy. In a night or so. It would be a mere game for our fellows; it's what they're made for. . . . Guns? Shrapnel and stuff wouldn't stop good men who meant business."

"Why don't *they* do that?"

"Their men aren't brutes enough: that's the trouble. They're a crowd of devitalized townsmen, and that's the truth of the matter. They're clerks, they're factory hands, they're students, they're civilized men. They can write, they can talk, they can make and do all sorts of things, but they're poor amateurs at war. They've got no physical staying power, and that's the whole thing. They've never slept in the open one night in their lives; they've never drunk anything but the purest water-company water; they've never gone short of three meals a day since they left their feeding-bottles. Half their cavalry never cocked leg over horse till it enlisted six months ago. They ride their horses as though they were bicycles—you watch 'em! They're fools at the game, and they know it. Our boys of fourteen can give their grown men points. . . . Very well——"

The war correspondent mused on his face with his nose between his knuckles.

"If a decent civilization," he said, "cannot produce better men for war than——"

He stopped with belated politeness.

"I mean——"

"Than our open-air life," said the young lieutenant, politely.

"Exactly," said the war correspondent. "Then civilization has to stop."

"It looks like it," the young lieutenant admitted.

"Civilization has science, you know," said the war correspondent. "It invented and it makes the rifles and guns and things you use."

"Which our nice healthy hunters and stockmen and so on, rowdy-dowdy cowpunchers and negro-whackers, can use ten times better than——*What's that?*"

"What?" said the war correspondent, and then seeing his companion busy with his field-glass he produced his own. "Where?" said the war correspondent, sweeping the enemy's lines.

H. G. Wells

"It's nothing," said the young lieutenant, still looking.

"What's nothing?"

The young lieutenant put down his glass and pointed. "I thought I saw something there, behind the stems of those trees. Something black. What it was I don't know."

The war correspondent tried to get even by intense scrutiny.

"It wasn't anything," said the young lieutenant, rolling over to regard the darkling evening sky, and generalized: "There never will be anything any more for ever. Unless——"

The war correspondent looked inquiry.

"They may get their stomachs wrong, or something—living without proper drains."

A sound of bugles came from the tents behind. The war correspondent slid backward down the sand and stood up. "Boom!" came from somewhere far away to the left. "Halloa!" he said, hesitated, and crawled back to peer again. "Firing at this time is jolly bad manners."

The young lieutenant was incommunicative again for a space.

Then he pointed to the distant clump of trees again. "One of our big guns. They were firing at that," he said.

"The thing that wasn't anything?"

"Something over there, anyhow."

Both men were silent, peering through their glasses for a space. "Just when it's twilight," the lieutenant complained. He stood up.

"I might stay here a bit," said the war correspondent.

The lieutenant shook his head. "There is nothing to see," he apologized, and then went down to where his little squad of sun-brown, loose-limbed men had been yarning in the trench. The war correspondent stood up also, glanced for a moment at the business-like bustle below him, gave perhaps twenty seconds to those enigmatical trees again, then turned his face toward the camp.

He found himself wondering whether his editor would consider the story of how somebody thought he saw something black behind a clump of trees, and how a gun was fired at this illusion by somebody else, too trivial for public consultation.

"It's the only gleam of a shadow of interest," said the war correspondent, "for ten whole days."

"No," he said, presently; "I'll write that other article, 'Is War Played Out?'"

He surveyed the darkling lines in perspective, the tangle of trenches one behind another, one commanding another, which the defender had made ready. The shadows and mists swallowed up their receding contours, and here and there a lantern gleamed, and here and there knots of men were busy about small fires.

"No troops on earth could do it," he said. . . .

He was depressed. He believed that there were other things in life better worth having than proficiency in war; he believed that in the heart of civilization, for all its stresses, its crushing concentrations of forces, its injustice and suffering, there lay something that might be the hope of the world, and the idea that any people by living in the open air, hunting perpetually, losing touch with books and art and all the things that intensify life, might hope to resist and break that great development to the end of time, jarred on his civilized soul.

Apt to his thought came a file of defender soldiers and passed him in the gleam of a swinging lamp that marked the way.

He glanced at their red-lit faces, and one shone out for a moment, a common type of face in the defender's ranks: ill-shaped nose, sensuous lips, bright clear eyes full of alert cunning, slouch hat cocked on one side and adorned with the peacock's plume of the rustic Don Juan turned soldier, a hard brown skin, a sinewy frame, an open, tireless stride, and a master's grip on the rifle.

The war correspondent returned their salutations and went on his way.

"Louts," he whispered. "Cunning, elementary louts. And they are going to beat the townsmen at the game of war!"

From the red glow among the nearer tents came first one and then half-a-dozen hearty voices, bawling in a drawling unison the words of a particularly slab and sentimental patriotic song.

"Oh, *go* it!" muttered the war correspondent, bitterly.

II.

It was opposite the trenches called after Hackbone's Hut that the battle began. There the ground stretched broad and level between the lines, with scarcely shelter for a lizard, and it seemed to the startled, just awakened men who came crowding into the trenches that this was one more proof of that green inexperience of the enemy of which they had heard so much. The war correspondent would not believe his ears at first, and swore that he and the war artist, who, still imperfectly roused, was trying to put on his boots by the light of a match held in his hand, were the victims of a common illusion. Then, after putting his head in a bucket of cold water, his intelligence came back as he towelled. He listened. "Gollys!" he said; "that's something more than scare firing this time. It's like ten thousand carts on a bridge of tin."

There came a sort of enrichment to that steady uproar. "Machine-guns!"

Then, "Guns!"

The artist, with one boot on, thought to look at his watch, and went to it hopping.

"Half an hour from dawn," he said. "You were right about their attacking, after all. . . ."

The war correspondent came out of the tent, verifying the presence of chocolate in his pocket as he did so. He had to halt for a moment or so until his eyes were toned down to the night a little. "Pitch!" he said. He stood for a space to season his eyes before he felt justified in striking out for a black gap among the adjacent tents. The artist coming out behind him fell over a tent-rope. It was half-past two o'clock in the morning of the darkest night in time, and against a sky of dull black silk the enemy was talking searchlights, a wild jabber of searchlights. "He's trying to blind our riflemen," said the war correspondent with a flash, and waited for the artist and then set off with a sort of discreet haste again. "Whoa!" he said, presently. "Ditches!"

They stopped.

"It's the confounded searchlights," said the war correspondent.

They saw lanterns going to and fro, near by, and men falling in to march down to the trenches. They were for following them, and then the artist began to feel his night eyes. "If we scramble this," he said, "and it's only a drain, there's a clear run up to the ridge." And that way they took. Lights came and went in the tents behind, as the men turned out, and ever and again they came to broken ground and staggered and stumbled. But in a little while they drew near the crest. Something that sounded like the impact of a very important railway accident happened in the air above them, and the shrapnel bullets seethed about them like a sudden handful of hail. "Rightho!" said the war correspondent, and soon they judged they had come to the crest and stood in the midst of a world of great darkness and frantic glares, whose principal fact was sound.

Right and left of them and all about them was the uproar, an army-full of magazine fire, at first chaotic and monstrous and then, eked out by little flashes and gleams and suggestions, taking the beginnings of a shape. It looked to the war correspondent as though the enemy must have attacked in line and with his whole force—in which case he was either being or was already annihilated.

"Dawn and the dead," he said, with his instinct for headlines. He said this to himself, but afterwards, by means of shouting, he conveyed an idea to the artist.

"They must have meant it for a surprise," he said.

It was remarkable how the firing kept on. After a time he began to perceive a sort of rhythm in this inferno of noise. It would decline—decline perceptibly, droop towards something that was comparatively a pause—a pause of inquiry. "Aren't you all dead yet?" this pause seemed to say. The flickering fringe of rifle-flashes would become attenuated and broken, and the whack-bang of the enemy's big guns two miles away there would come up out of the deeps. Then suddenly, east or west of them, something would startle the rifles to a frantic outbreak again.

The war correspondent taxed his brain for some theory of conflict that would account for this, and was suddenly aware that the artist and he were vividly illuminated. He could see the ridge on which they stood and before them in black outline a file of riflemen hurrying down towards the nearer trenches. It became visible that a light rain was falling, and farther away towards the enemy was a clear space with men—"our men?"—running across it in disorder. He saw one of those men throw up his hands and drop. And something else black and shining loomed up on the edge of the beam-coruscating flashes; and behind it and far away a calm, white eye regarded the world. "Whit, whit, whit," sang something in the air, and then the artist was running for cover, with the war correspondent behind him. Bang came shrapnel, bursting close at hand as it seemed, and our two men were lying flat in a dip in the ground, and the light and everything had gone again, leaving a vast note of interrogation upon the night.

The war correspondent came within bawling range. "What the deuce was it? Shooting our men down!"

H. G. Wells

"Black," said the artist, "and like a fort. Not two hundred yards from the first trench."

He sought for comparisons in his mind. "Something between a big blockhouse and a giant's dish-cover," he said.

"And they were running!" said the war correspondent.

"*You'd* run if a thing like that, searchlight to help it, turned up like a prowling nightmare in the middle of the night."

They crawled to what they judged the edge of the dip and lay regarding the unfathomable dark. For a space they could distinguish nothing, and then a sudden convergence of the searchlights of both sides brought the strange thing out again.

In that flickering pallor it had the effect of a large and clumsy black insect, an insect the size of an ironclad cruiser, crawling obliquely to the first line of trenches and firing shots out of portholes in its side. And on its carcass the bullets must have been battering with more than the passionate violence of hail on a roof of tin.

Then in the twinkling of an eye the curtain of the dark had fallen again and the monster had vanished, but the crescendo of musketry marked its approach to the trenches.

They were beginning to talk about the thing to each other, when a flying bullet kicked dirt into the artist's face, and they decided abruptly to crawl down into the cover of the trenches. They had got down with an unobtrusive persistence into the second line, before the dawn had grown clear enough for anything to be seen. They found themselves in a crowd of expectant riflemen, all noisily arguing about what would happen next. The enemy's contrivance had done execution upon the outlying men, it seemed, but they did not believe it would do any more. "Come the day and we'll capture the lot of them," said a burly soldier.

"Them?" said the war correspondent.

"They say there's a regular string of 'em, crawling along the front of our lines. . . . Who cares?"

The darkness filtered away so imperceptibly that at no moment could one declare decisively that one could see. The searchlights ceased to sweep hither and thither. The enemy's monsters were dubious patches of darkness upon the dark, and then no longer dubious, and so they crept out into distinctness. The war correspondent, munching chocolate absent-mindedly, beheld at last a spacious picture of battle under the cheerless sky, whose central focus was an array of fourteen or fifteen huge clumsy shapes lying in perspective on the very edge of the first line of trenches, at intervals of perhaps three hundred yards, and evidently firing down upon the crowded riflemen. They were so close in that the defender's guns had ceased, and only the first line of trenches was in action.

The second line commanded the first, and as the light grew the war correspondent could make out the riflemen who were fighting these monsters, crouched in knots and crowds behind the transverse banks that crossed the trenches against the eventuality of an enfilade. The trenches close to the big machines were empty save for the crumpled suggestions of dead and wounded men; the defenders had been driven right and left as soon as the prow of this land ironclad had loomed up over the front of the trench. He produced his field-glass, and was immediately a centre of inquiry from the soldiers about him.

They wanted to look, they asked questions, and after he had announced that the men across the traverses seemed unable to advance or retreat, and were crouching under cover rather than fighting, he found it advisable to loan his glasses to a burly and incredulous corporal. He heard a strident voice, and found a lean and sallow soldier at his back talking to the artist.

"There's chaps down there caught," the man was saying. "If they retreat they got to expose themselves, and the fire's too straight. . . ."

"They aren't firing much, but every shot's a hit."

"Who?"

"The chaps in that thing. The men who're coming up——"

"Coming up where?"

"We're evacuating them trenches where we can. Our chaps are coming back up the zigzags. . . . No end of 'em hit. . . . But when we get clear our turn'll come. Rather! These things won't be able to cross a trench or get into it; and before they can get back our guns'll smash 'em up. Smash 'em right up. See?" A brightness came into his eyes. "Then we'll have a go at the beggar inside," he said. . . .

The war correspondent thought for a moment, trying to realize the idea. Then he set himself to recover his field-glasses from the burly corporal. . . .

The daylight was getting clearer now. The clouds were lifting, and a gleam of lemon-yellow amidst the level masses to the east portended sunrise. He looked again at the land ironclad. As he saw it in the bleak grey dawn, lying obliquely upon the slope and on the very lip of the foremost trench, the suggestion of a stranded vessel was very great indeed. It might have been from eighty to a hundred feet long—it was about two hundred and fifty yards away—its vertical side was ten feet high or so, smooth for that height, and then with a complex patterning under the eaves of its flattish turtle cover. This patterning was a close interlacing of portholes, rifle barrels, and telescope tubes—sham and real—indistinguishable one from the other. The thing had come into such a position as to enfilade the trench, which was empty now, so far as he could see, except for two or three crouching knots of men and the tumbled dead. Behind it, across the plain, it had scored the grass with a train of linked impressions, like the dotted tracings sea-things leave in sand. Left and right of that track dead men and wounded men were scattered—men it had picked off as they fled back from their advanced positions in the searchlight glare from the invader's lines. And now it lay with its head projecting a little over the trench it had won, as if it were a single sentient thing planning the next phase of its attack. . . .

He lowered his glasses and took a more comprehensive view of the situation. These creatures of the night had evidently won the first line of trenches and the fight had come to a pause. In the increasing light he could make out by a stray shot or a chance exposure that the defender's marksmen were lying thick in the second and third line of trenches up towards the low crest of the position, and in such of the zigzags as gave them a chance of a converging fire. The men about him were talking of guns. "We're in the line of the big guns at the crest but they'll soon shift one to pepper them," the lean man said, reassuringly.

"Whup," said the corporal:

"Bang! bang! bang! Whir-r-r-r-r!" It was a sort of nervous jump, and all the rifles were going off by themselves. The war correspondent found himself and the artist, two idle men crouching behind a line of preoccupied backs, of industrious men discharging magazines. The monster had moved. It continued to move regardless of the hail that splashed its skin with bright new specks of lead. It was singing a mechanical little ditty to itself, "Tuf-tuf, tuf-tuf, tuf-tuf," and squirting out little jets of steam behind. It had humped itself up, as a limpet does before it crawls; it had lifted its skirt and displayed along the length of it— feet! They were thick, stumpy feet, between knobs and buttons in shape—flat, broad things, reminding one of the feet of elephants or the legs of caterpillars; and then, as the skirt rose higher, the war correspondent, scrutinizing the thing through his glasses again, saw that these feet hung, as it were, on the rims of wheels. His thoughts whirled back to Victoria Street, Westminster, and he saw himself in the piping times of peace, seeking matter for an interview.

"Mr.—Mr. Diplock," he said; "and he called them Pedrails. . . . Fancy meeting them here!"

The marksman beside him raised his head and shoulders in a speculative mood to fire more certainly—it seemed so natural to assume the attention of the monster must be distracted by this trench before it—and was suddenly knocked backwards by a bullet through his neck. His feet flew up, and he vanished out of the margin of the watcher's field of vision. The war correspondent grovelled tighter, but after a glance behind him at a painful little confusion, he resumed his field-glass, for the thing was putting down its feet one after the other, and hoisting itself farther and farther over the trench. Only a bullet in the head could have stopped him looking just then.

The lean man with the strident voice ceased firing to turn and reiterate his point. "They can't possibly cross," he bawled. "They——"

"Bang! Bang! Bang! Bang!"—drowned everything.

The lean man continued speaking for a word or so, then gave it up, shook his head to enforce the impossibility of anything crossing a trench like the one below, and resumed business once more.

And all the while that great bulk was crossing. When the war correspondent turned his glass on it again it had bridged the trench, and its queer feet were rasping away at the farther bank, in the attempt to get a hold there. It got its hold. It continued to crawl until the greater bulk of it was over the trench—until it was all over. Then it paused for a moment, adjusted its skirt a little nearer the ground, gave an unnerving "toot, toot," and came on abruptly at a pace of, perhaps, six miles an hour straight up the gentle slope towards our observer.

The war correspondent raised himself on his elbow and looked a natural inquiry at the artist.

For a moment the men about him stuck to their position and fired furiously. Then the lean man in a mood of precipitancy slid backwards, and the war correspondent said "Come along" to the artist, and led the movement along the trench.

As they dropped down, the vision of a hillside of trench being rushed by a dozen vast cockroaches disappeared for a space, and instead was one of a narrow passage, crowded with men, for the most part receding, though one or two turned or halted. He never turned back to see the nose of the monster creep over the brow of the trench; he never even troubled to keep in touch with the artist. He heard the "whit" of bullets about him soon enough, and saw a man before him stumble and drop, and then he was one of a furious crowd fighting to get into a transverse zigzag ditch that enabled the defenders to get under cover up and down the hill. It was like a theatre panic. He gathered from signs and fragmentary words that on ahead another of these monsters had also won to the second trench.

He lost his interest in the general course of the battle for a space altogether; he became simply a modest egotist, in a mood of hasty circumspection, seeking the farthest rear, amidst a dispersed multitude of disconcerted riflemen similarly employed. He scrambled down through trenches, he took his courage in both hands and sprinted across the open, he had moments of panic when it seemed madness not to be quadrupedal, and moments of shame when he stood up and faced about to see how the fight was going. And he was one of many thousand very similar men that morning. On the ridge he halted in a knot of scrub, and was for a few minutes almost minded to stop and see things out.

The day was now fully come. The grey sky had changed to blue, and of all the cloudy masses of the dawn there remained only a few patches of dissolving fleeciness. The world below was bright and singularly clear. The ridge was not, perhaps, more than a hundred feet or so above the general plain, but in this flat region it sufficed to give the effect of extensive view. Away on the north side of the ridge, little and far, were the camps, the ordered wagons, all the gear of a big army; with officers galloping about and men doing aimless things. Here and there men were falling in, however and the cavalry was forming up on the plain beyond the tents. The bulk of men who had been in the trenches were still on the move to the rear, scattered like sheep without a shepherd over the farther slopes. Here and there were little rallies and attempts to wait and do—something vague; but the general drift was away from any concentration. There on the southern side was the elaborate lacework of trenches and defences, across which these iron turtles, fourteen of them spread out over a line of perhaps three miles, were now advancing as fast as a man could trot, and methodically shooting down and breaking up any persistent knots of resistance. Here and there stood little clumps of men, outflanked and unable to get away, showing the white flag, and the invader's cyclist-infantry was advancing now across the open, in open order but unmolested, to complete the work of the machines. Surveyed at large, the defenders already looked a beaten army. A mechanism that was effectually ironclad against bullets, that could at a pinch cross a thirty-foot trench, and that seemed able to shoot out rifle-bullets with unerring precision, was clearly an inevitable victor against anything but rivers, precipices, and guns.

He looked at his watch. "Half-past four! Lord! What things can happen in two hours. Here's the whole blessed army being walked over, and at half-past two——"

"And even now our blessed louts haven't done a thing with their guns!"

He scanned the ridge right and left of him with his glasses. He turned again to the nearest land ironclad, advancing now obliquely to him and not three hundred yards away, and then scrambled the ground over which he must retreat if he was not to be captured.

"They'll do nothing," he said, and glanced again at the enemy.

And then from far away to the left came the thud of a gun, followed very rapidly by a rolling gunfire.

He hesitated and decided to stay.

III.

The defender had relied chiefly upon his rifles in the event of an assault. His guns he kept concealed at various points upon and behind the ridge ready to bring them into action against any artillery preparations for an attack on the part of his antagonist. The situation had rushed upon him with the dawn, and by the time the gunners had their guns ready for motion, the land ironclads were already in among the foremost trenches. There is a natural reluctance to fire into one's own broken men, and many of the guns, being intended simply to fight an advance of the enemy's artillery, were not in positions to hit anything in the second line of trenches. After that the advance of the land ironclads was swift. The defender-general found himself suddenly called upon to invent a new sort of warfare, in which guns were to fight alone amidst broken and retreating infantry. He had scarcely thirty minutes in which to think it out. He did not respond to the call, and what happened that morning was that the advance of the land ironclads forced the fight, and each gun and battery made what play its circumstances dictated. For the most part it was poor play.

Some of the guns got in two or three shots, some one or two, and the percentage of misses was unusually high. The howitzers, of course, did nothing. The land ironclads in each case followed much the same tactics. As soon as a gun came into play the monster turned itself almost end on, so as to minimize the chances of a square hit, and made not for the gun, but for the nearest point on its flank from which the gunners could be shot down. Few of the hits scored were very effectual; only one of the things was disabled, and that was the one that fought the three batteries attached to the brigade on the left wing. Three that were hit when close upon the guns were clean shot through without being put out of action. Our war correspondent did not see that one momentary arrest of the tide of victory on the left; he saw only the very ineffectual fight of half-battery 96B close at hand upon his right. This he watched some time beyond the margin of safety.

Just after he heard the three batteries opening up upon his left he became aware of the thud of horses' hoofs from the sheltered side of the slope, and presently saw first one and then two other guns galloping into position along the north side of the ridge, well out of sight of the great bulk that was now creeping obliquely towards the crest and cutting up the lingering infantry beside it and below, as it came.

The half-battery swung round into line—each gun describing its curve—halted, unlimbered, and prepared for action. . . .

"Bang!"

The land ironclad had become visible over the brow of the hill, and just visible as a long black back to the gunners. It halted, as though it hesitated.

The two remaining guns fired, and then their big antagonist had swung round and was in full view, end on, against the sky, coming at a rush.

The gunners became frantic in their haste to fire again. They were so near the war correspondent could see the expressions on their excited faces through his field-glass. As he looked he saw a man drop, and realized for the first time that the ironclad was shooting.

For a moment the big black monster crawled with an accelerated pace towards the furiously active gunners. Then, as if moved by a generous impulse, it turned its full broadside to their attack, and scarcely forty yards away from them. The war correspondent turned his field-glass back to the gunners and perceived it was now shooting down the men about the guns with the most deadly rapidity.

Just for a moment it seemed splendid and then it seemed horrible. The gunners were dropping in heaps about their guns. To lay a hand on a gun was death. "Bang!" went the gun on the left, a hopeless miss, and that was the only second shot the half-battery fired. In another moment half-a-dozen surviving artillerymen were holding up their hands amidst a scattered muddle of dead and wounded men, and the fight was done.

The war correspondent hesitated between stopping in his scrub and waiting for an opportunity to surrender decently, or taking to an adjacent gully he had discovered. If he surrendered it was certain he would get no copy off; while, if he escaped, there were all sorts of chances. He decided to follow the gully, and take the first offer in the confusion beyond the camp of picking up a horse.

IV.

Subsequent authorities have found fault with the first land ironclads in many particulars, but assuredly they served their purpose on the day of their appearance. They were essentially long, narrow, and very strong steel frameworks carrying the engines, and borne upon eight pairs of big pedrail wheels, each about ten feet in diameter, each a driving wheel and set upon long axles free to swivel round a common axis. This arrangement gave them the maximum of adaptability to the contours of the ground. They crawled level along the ground with one foot high upon a hillock and another deep in a depression, and they could hold themselves erect and steady sideways upon even a steep hillside. The engineers directed the engines under the command of the captain, who had look-out points at small ports all round the upper edge of the adjustable skirt of twelve-inch iron-plating which protected the whole affair, and could also raise or depress a conning-tower set about the portholes through the center of the iron top cover. The riflemen each occupied a small cabin of peculiar construction and these cabins were slung along the sides of and before and behind the great main framework, in a manner suggestive of the slinging of the seats of an Irish jaunting-car. Their rifles, however, were very different pieces of apparatus from the simple mechanisms in the hands of their adversaries.

These were in the first place automatic, ejected their cartridges and loaded again from a magazine each time they fired, until the ammunition store was at an end, and they had the most remarkable sights imaginable, sights which threw a bright little camera-obscura picture into the light-tight box in which the rifleman sat below. This camera-obscura picture was marked with two crossed lines, and whatever was covered by the intersection of these two lines, that the rifle hit. The sighting was ingeniously contrived. The rifleman stood at the table with a thing like an elaborately of a draughtsman's dividers in his hand, and he opened and closed these dividers, so that they were always at the apparent height—if it was an ordinary-sized man—of the man he wanted to kill. A little twisted strand of wire like an electric-light wire ran from this implement up to the gun, and as the dividers opened and shut the sights went up and down. Changes in the clearness of the atmosphere, due to changes of moisture, were met by an ingenious use of that meteorologically sensitive substance, catgut, and when the land ironclad moved forward the sites got a compensatory deflection in the direction of its motion. The rifleman stood up in his pitch-dark chamber and watched the little picture before him. One hand held the dividers for judging distance, and the other grasped a big knob like a door-handle. As he pushed this knob about the rifle above swung to correspond, and the picture passed to and fro like an agitated panorama. When he saw a man he wanted to shoot he brought him up to the cross-lines, and then pressed a finger upon a little push like an electric bell-push, conveniently placed in the center of the knob. Then the man was shot. If by any chance the rifleman missed his target he moved the knob a trifle, or readjusted his dividers, pressed the push, and got him the second time.

This rifle and its sights protruded from a porthole, exactly like a great number of other portholes that ran in a triple row under the eaves of the cover of the land ironclad. Each porthole displayed a rifle and sight in dummy, so that the real ones could only be hit by a chance shot, and if one was, then the young man below said "Pshaw!" turned on an electric light, lowered the injured instrument into his camera, replaced the injured part, or put up a new rifle if the injury was considerable.

You must conceive these cabins as hung clear above the swing of the axles, and inside the big wheels upon which the great elephant-like feet were hung, and behind these cabins along the center of the monster ran a central gallery into which they opened, and along which worked the big compact engines. It was like a long passage into which this throbbing machinery had been packed, and the captain stood about the middle, close to the ladder that led to his conning-tower, and directed the silent, alert engineers—for the most part by signs. The throb and noise of the engines mingled with the reports of the rifles and the intermittent clangour of the bullet hail upon the armour. Ever and again he would touch the wheel that raised his conning tower, step up his ladder until his engineers could see nothing of him above the waist, and then come down again with orders. Two small electric lights were all the illumination of this space—they were placed to make him most clearly visible to his subordinates; the air was thick with the smell of oil and petrol, and had the war correspondent been suddenly transferred from the spacious dawn outside to the bowels of the apparatus he would have thought himself fallen into another world.

The captain, of course, saw both sides of the battle. When he raised his head into his conning-tower there were the dewy sunrise, the amazed and disordered trenches, the flying and falling soldiers, the depressed-looking groups of prisoners, the beaten guns; when he bent down again to signal "half speed," "quarter speed," "half circle round towards the right," or what not, he was in the oil-smelling twilight of the ill-lit engine room. Close beside him on either side was the mouthpiece of a speaking-tube, and ever and again he would direct one side or other of his strange craft to "Concentrate fire forward on gunners," or to "clear out trench about a hundred yards on our right front."

He was a young man, healthy enough but by no means sun-tanned, and of a type of feature and expression that prevails in His Majesty's Navy: alert, intelligent, quiet. He and his engineers and his riflemen all went about their work, calm and reasonable men. They had none of that flapping strenuousness of the half-wit in a hurry, that excessive strain upon the blood-vessels, that hysteria of effort which is so frequently regarded as the proper state of mind for heroic deeds.

For the enemy these young engineers were defeating they felt a certain qualified pity and a quite unqualified contempt. They regarded these big, healthy men they were shooting down precisely as these same big, healthy men might regard some inferior kind of native. They despised them for making war; despised their bawling patriotisms and their emotionality profoundly; despised them, above all, for the petty cunning and the almost brutish want of imagination their method of fighting displayed. "If they *must* make war," these young men thought, "why in thunder don't they do it like sensible men?" They resented the assumption that their own side was too stupid to do anything more than play their enemy's game, that they were going to play this costly folly according to the rules of unimaginative men. They resented being forced to the trouble of making man-killing machinery; resented the alternative of having to massacre these people or endure their truculent yappings; resented the whole unfathom-able imbecility of war.

Meanwhile, with something of the mechanical precision of a good clerk posting a ledger, the riflemen moved their knobs and pressed their buttons. . . .

The captain of Land Ironclad Number Three had halted on the crest close to his captured half-battery. His lined-up prisoners stood hard by and waited for the cyclists behind to come for them. He surveyed the victorious morning through his conning-tower.

He read the general's signals. "Five and Four are to keep among the guns to the left and prevent any attempt to recover them. Seven and Eleven and Twelve, stick to the guns you have got; Seven, get into position to command the guns taken by Three. Then, we're to do something else, are we? Six and One, quicken up to about ten miles an hour and walk round behind that camp to the levels near the river—we shall bag the whole crowd of them," interjected the young man. "Ah, here we are! Two and Three, Eight and Nine, Thirteen and Fourteen, space out to a thousand yards, wait for the word, and then go slowly to cover the advance of the cyclist infantry against any charge of mounted troops. That's all right. But where's Ten? Halloa! Ten to repair and get movable as soon as possible. They've broken up Ten!"

The discipline of the new war machines was business-like rather than pedantic, and the head of the captain came down out of the conning-tower to tell his men. "I say, you chaps there. They've broken up Ten. Not badly, I think; but anyhow, he's stuck."

But that still left thirteen of the monsters in action to finish up the broken army.

The war correspondent stealing down his gully looked back and saw them all lying along the crest and talking fluttering congratulatory flags to one another. Their iron sides were shining golden in the light of the rising sun.

V.

The private adventures of the war correspondent terminated in surrender about one o'clock in the afternoon, and by that time he had stolen a horse, pitched off it, and narrowly escaped being rolled upon; found the brute had broken its leg, and shot it with his revolver. He had spent some hours in the company of a squad of dispirited riflemen, had quarrelled with them about topography at last, and gone off by himself in a direction that should have brought him to the banks of the river and didn't. Moreover, he had eaten all his chocolate and found nothing in the whole world to drink. Also, it had become extremely hot. From behind a broken, but attractive, stone wall he had seen far away in the distance the defender-horsemen trying to charge cyclists in open order, with land ironclads outflanking them on either side. He had discovered that cyclists could retreat over open turf before horsemen with a sufficient margin of speed to allow of frequent dismounts and much terribly effective sharpshooting; and he had a sufficient persuasion that those horsemen, having charged their hearts out, had halted just beyond his range of vision and surrendered. He had been urged to sudden activity by a forward movement of one of those machines that had threatened to enfilade his wall. He had discovered a fearful blister on his heel.

He was now in a scrubby gravelly place, sitting down and meditating on his pocket-handkerchief, which had in some extraordinary way become in the last twenty-four hours extremely ambiguous in hue. "It's the whitest thing I've got," he said.

He had known all along that the enemy was east, west, and south of him, but when he heard war ironclads Numbers One and Six talking in their measured, deadly way not half a mile to the north he decided to make his own little unconditional peace without any further risks. He was for hoisting his white flag to a bush and taking up a position of modest obscurity near it, until someone came along. He became aware of voices, clatter, and the distinctive noises of a body of horse, quite near, and he put his handkerchief in his pocket again and went to see what was going forward.

The sound of firing ceased, and then as he drew near he heard the deep sounds of many simple, coarse, but hearty and noble-hearted soldiers of the old school swearing with vigour.

He emerged from his scrub upon a big level plain, and far away a fringe of trees marked the banks of the river. In the center of the picture was a still intact road bridge, and a big railway bridge a little to the right. Two land ironclads rested, with a general air of being long, harmless sheds, in a pose of anticipatory peacefulness right and left of the picture, completely commanding two miles and more of the river levels. Emerged and halted a few yards from the scrub was the remainder of the defender's cavalry, dusty, a little disordered and obviously annoyed, but still a very fine show of men. In the middle distance three or four men and horses were receiving medical attendance, and nearer a knot of officers regarded the distant novelties in mechanism with profound distaste. Everyone was very distinctly aware of the twelve other ironclads, and of the multitude of townsmen soldiers, on bicycles or afoot, encumbered now by prisoners and captured war-gear but otherwise thoroughly effective, who were sweeping like a great net in their rear.

"Checkmate," said the war correspondent, walking out into the open. "But I surrender in the best of company. Twenty-four hours ago I thought war was impossible— and these beggars have captured the whole blessed army! Well! Well!" He thought of his talk with the young lieutenant. "If there's no end to the surprises of science, the civilized people have it, of course. As long as their science keeps going they will necessarily be ahead of open-country men. Still. . . ." He wondered for a space what might have happened to the young lieutenant.

The war correspondent was one of those inconsistent people who always want the beaten side to win. When he saw all these burly, sun-tanned horsemen, disarmed and dismounted and lined up; when he saw their horses unskillfully led away by the singularly not equestrian cyclists to whom they had surrendered; when he saw these truncated Paladins watching this scandalous sight, he forgot altogether that he had called these men "cunning louts" and wished them beaten not four-and-twenty

H. G. Wells

hours ago. A month ago he had seen that regiment in its pride going forth to war, and had been told of its terrible prowess, how it could charge in open order with each man firing from his saddle, and sweep before it anything else that ever came out to battle in any sort of order, foot or horse. And it had had to fight a few score of young men in atrociously unfair machines!

"Manhood *versus* Machinery" occurred to him as a suitable headline. Journalism curdles all one's mind to phrases.

He strolled as near the lined-up prisoners as the sentinels seemed disposed to permit and surveyed them and compared their sturdy proportions with those of their lightly built captors.

"Smart degenerates," he muttered. "Anæmic cockneydom."

The surrendered officers came quite close to him presently, and he could hear the colonel's high-pitched tenor. The poor gentleman had spent three years of arduous toil upon the best material in the world perfecting that shooting from the saddle charge, and he was mourning with phrases of blasphemy, natural under the circumstances what one could be expected to do against this suitably consigned ironmongery.

"Guns," said some one.

"Big guns they can walk round. You can't shift big guns to keep pace with them and little guns in the open they rush. I saw 'em rushed. You might do a surprise now and then—assassinate the brutes, perhaps——"

"You might make things like 'em."

"What? *More* ironmongery? Us?. . . ."

"I'll call my article," meditated the war correspondent, "'Mankind *versus* Ironmongery,' and quote the old boy at the beginning."

And he was much too good a journalist to spoil his contrast by remarking that the half-dozen comparatively slender young men in blue pajamas who were standing about their victorious land ironclad, drinking coffee and eating biscuits, had also in their eyes and carriage something not altogether degraded below the level of a man.

1903

THE REPUBLIC OF THE SOUTHERN CROSS

Valery Bryusov

There have appeared lately a whole series of descriptions of the dreadful catastrophe which has overtaken the Republic of the Southern Cross. They are strikingly various, and give many details of a manifestly fantastic and improbable character. Evidently the writers of these descriptions have lent a too ready ear to the narratives of the survivors from Star City (*Zvezdny*), the inhabitants of which, as is common knowledge, were all stricken with a psychical distemper. For that reason we consider it opportune to give an account here of all the reliable evidence which we have as yet of this tragedy of the Southern Pole.

The Republic of the Southern Cross came into being some forty years ago, as a development from three hundred steel works established in the Southern Polar regions. In a circular note sent to each and every Government of the whole world, the new state expressed its pretensions to all lands, whether mainland or island, within the limits of the Antarctic circle, as also all parts of these lands stretching beyond the line. It announced its readiness to purchase from the various other states affected the lands which they considered to be under their special protectorate. The pretensions of the new Republic did not meet with any opposition on the part of the fifteen great powers of the world. Debatable points concerning certain islands lying entirely outside the Polar circle, but closely related to the Southern Polar state were settled by special treaties. On the fulfilment of the various formalities the Republic of the Southern Cross was received into the family of world states, and its representatives were recognised by all Governments.

The chief city of the Republic, having the name of Zvezdny, was situated at the actual Pole itself. At that imaginary point where the earth's axis passes and all earthly meridians become one, stood the Town Hall, and the roof with its pointed towers looked upon the nadir of the heavens. The streets of the town extended along meridians from the Town Hall and these meridians were intersected by other streets in concentric circles. The height of all the buildings was the same, as was also their external appearance. There were no windows in the walls, as all the houses were lit by electricity and the streets were lighted by electricity. Because of the severity of the climate, an impenetrable and opaque roof had been built over the town, with powerful ventilators for a constant change of air. These localities of the globe have but one day in six months, and one long night also of six months, but the streets of Zvezdny were always lighted by a bright and even light. In the same way in all seasons of the year the temperature of the streets was kept at one and the same height.

According to the last census the population of Zvezdny had reached two and a half millions. The whole of the remaining population of the Republic, numbering fifty millions, were concentrated in the neighbourhood of the ports and factories. These other points were also marked by the settlement of millions of people in towns which in external characteristics were reminiscent of Zvezdny. Thanks to a clever application of electric power, the entrance to the local havens remained open all the year round. Overhead electric railways connected the most populated parts of the Republic, and every day tens of thousands of people and millions of kilogrammes of material passed along these roads from one town to another. The interior of the country remained uninhabited. Travellers looking out of the train window saw before them only monotonous wildernesses, white in winter, and overgrown with wretched grass during the three months of summer. Wild animals had long since been destroyed, and for human beings there was no means of sustenance. More remarkable was the hustling life of the ports and industrial centres. In order to give some understanding of the life, it is perhaps enough to say that of late years about seven-tenths of the whole of the world's output of metal has come from the State mines of the Republic.

The constitution of the Republic, according to outward signs, appeared to be the realisation of extreme democracy. The only fully enfranchised citizens were the metal-workers, who numbered about sixty per cent of the whole population. The factories and mines were State property. The life of the miners was facilitated by all possible conveniences, and even with luxury. At their disposal, apart from magnificent accommodation and a *recherché* cuisine, were various educational institutions and means of amusement: libraries, museums, theatres, concerts, halls for all types of sport, etc. The number of working hours in the day were small in the extreme. The training and teaching of children, the giving of medical and legal aid, and the ministry of the various religious cults were all taken upon itself by the State. Ample provision for all the needs and even whims of the workmen of the State factories having been made, no wages whatever were paid; but families of citizens who had served twenty years in a factory, or who in their years of service had died or become enfeebled, received a handsome life pension on condition that they did not leave the Republic. From the workmen, by universal ballot, the representatives of the Law-making Chamber of the Republic were elected, and this Chamber had cognisance of all the questions of the political life of the country, being, however, without power to alter its fundamental laws.

It must be said that this democratic exterior concealed the purely autocratic tyranny of the shareholders and directors of a former Trust. Giving up to others the places of deputies in the Chamber they inevitably brought in their own candidates as directors of the factories. In the hands of the Board of Directors was concentrated the economic life of the country. The directors received all the orders and assigned them to the various factories for fulfilment; they purchased the materials and the machines for the work; they managed the whole business of the factories. Through their hands passed immense sums of money, to be reckoned in milliards. The Law-making Chamber only certified the entries of debits and credits in the upkeep of the factories, the accounts being handed to it for that purpose, and the balance on these accounts greatly exceeded the whole budget of the Republic. The influence of the Board of Directors in the international relationships of the Republic was immense. Its decisions might ruin whole countries. The prices fixed by them determined the wages of millions of labouring masses over the whole earth. And, moreover, the influence of the Board, though indirect, was always decisive in the internal affairs of the Republic. The Law-making Chamber, in fact, appeared to be only the humble servant of the will of the Board.

For the preservation of power in its own hands the Board was obliged to regulate mercilessly the whole life of the country. Though appearing to have liberty, the life of the citizens was standardised even to the most minute details. The buildings of all the towns of the Republic were according to one and the same pattern fixed by law. The decoration of all buildings used by the workmen, though luxurious to a degree, were strictly uniform. All received exactly the same food at exactly the same time. The clothes given out from the Government stores were unchanging and in the course of tens of years were of one and the same cut. At a signal from the Town Hall, at a definite hour, it was forbidden to go out of the houses. The whole Press of the country was subject to a sharp censorship. No articles directed against the dictatorship of the Board were allowed to see light. But, as a matter of fact, the whole country was so convinced of the benefit of this dictatorship that the compositors themselves would have refused to set the type of articles criticising the Board. The factories were full of the Board's spies. At the slightest manifestation of discontent with the Board the spies hastened to arrange meetings and dissuade the doubters with passionate speeches. The fact that the life of the workmen of the Republic was the object of the envy of the entire world was of course a disarming argument. It is said that in cases of continued agitation by certain individuals the Board did not hesitate to resort to political murder. In any case, during the whole existence of the Republic, the universal ballot of the citizens never brought to power one representative who was hostile to the directors.

The population of Zvezdny was composed chiefly of workmen who had served their time. They were, so to speak, Government shareholders. The means which they received from the State allowed them to live richly. It is not astonishing, therefore, that Zvezdny was reckoned one of the gayest cities of the world. For various *entrepreneurs* and entertainers it was a goldmine. The celebrities of the world brought hither their talents. Here were the best operas, best concerts, best exhibitions; here were brought out the best-informed gazettes. The shops of Zvezdny amazed by the richness of their choice of goods; the restaurants by the luxury and the delicacy of their service. Resorts of evil, where all forms of debauch invented in either the ancient or the modern world were to be found, abounded. However, the governmental regulation of life was preserved in Zvezdny also. It is true that the decorations of lodgings and the fashions of dress were not compulsorily determined, but the law forbidding the exit from the house after a certain hour remained in force, a strict censorship of the Press was maintained, and many spies were kept by the Board. Order was officially maintained by the popular police, but at the same time there existed the secret police of the all-cognisant Board. Such was in its general character the system of life in the Republic of the Southern Cross and in its capital. The problem of the future historian will be to determine how much this system was responsible for the outbreak and spread of that fatal disease which brought to destruction the town of Zvezdny, and with it, perhaps, the whole young Republic.

The first cases of the disease of "contradiction" were observed in the Republic some twenty years ago. It had then the character of a rare and sporadic malady. Nevertheless, the local mental experts were much interested by it and gave a circumstantial account of the symptoms at the international medical congress at Lhasa, where several reports of it were read. Later, it was somehow or other forgotten, though in the mental hospitals of Zvezdny there never was any difficulty in finding examples. The disease received its name from the fact that the victims continuously contradicted their wishes by their actions, wishing one thing but saying and doing another. [The scientific name of the disease is *mania contradicens*.] It begins with fairly feeble symptoms, generally those of characteristic aphasia. The stricken, instead of saying "yes," say "no"; wishing to say caressing words, they splutter abuse, etc. The majority also begin to contradict themselves in their behaviour; intending to go to the left they turn to the right, thinking to raise the brim of a hat so as to see better they would pull it down over their eyes instead, and so on. As the disease develops, contradiction overtakes the whole of the bodily and spiritual life of the patient, exhibiting infinite diversity conformable with the idiosyncrasies of each. In general, the speech of the patient becomes unintelligible and his actions absurd. The normality of the physiological functions of the organism is disturbed. Acknowledging the unwisdom of his behaviour the patient gets into a state of extreme excitement bordering even upon insanity. Many commit suicide, sometimes in fits of madness, sometimes in moments of spiritual brightness. Others perish from a rush of blood to the brain. In almost all cases the disease is mortal; cases of recovery are extremely rare.

The epidemic character was taken by *mania contradicens* during the middle months of this year in Zvezdny. Up till this time the number of cases had never exceeded two per cent of the total number of patients in the hospitals. But this proportion suddenly rose to twenty-five per cent during the month of May (autumn month, as it is called in the Republic), and it continued to increase during the succeeding months with as great rapidity. By the middle of June there were already two per cent of the whole population, that is, about fifty thousand people, officially notified as suffering from "contradiction." We have no statistical details of any later date. The hospitals overflowed. The doctors on the spot proved to be altogether insufficient. And, moreover, the doctors themselves, and the nurses in the hospitals, caught the disease also.

There was very soon no one to whom to appeal for medical aid, and a correct register of patients became impossible. The evidence given by eyewitnesses, however, is in agreement on this point, that it was impossible to find a family in which someone was not suffering. The number of healthy people rapidly decreased as panic caused a wholesale exodus from the town, but the number of the stricken increased. It is probably true that in the month of August all who had remained in Zvezdny were down with this psychical malady.

It is possible to follow the first developments of the epidemic by the columns of the local newspapers, headed in ever larger type as the mania grew. Since the detection of the disease in its early stages was very difficult, the chronicle of the first days of the epidemic is full of comic episodes. A train conductor on the metropolitan railway, instead of receiving money from the passengers, himself pays them. A policeman, whose duty it was to regulate the traffic, confuses it all day long. A visitor to a gallery, walking from room to room, turns all the pictures with their faces to the wall. A newspaper page of proof, being corrected by the hand of a reader already overtaken by the disease, is printed next morning full of the most amusing absurdities. At a concert, a sick violinist suddenly interrupts the harmonious efforts of the orchestra with the most dreadful dissonances. A whole long series of such happenings gave plenty of scope for the wits of local journalists. But several instances of a different type of phenomenon caused the jokes to come to a sudden end. The first was that a doctor overtaken by the disease prescribed poison for a girl patient in his care and she perished. For three days the newspapers were taken up with this circumstance. Then two nurses walking in the town gardens were overtaken by "contradiction," and cut the throats of forty-one children. This event staggered the whole city. But on the evening of the same day two victims fired the *mitrailleuse* from the quarters of the town militia and killed and injured some five hundred people.

At that, all the newspapers and the society of the town cried for prompt measures against the epidemic. At a special session of the combined Board and Legal Chamber it was decided to invite doctors from other towns and from abroad, to enlarge the existing hospitals, to build new ones, and to construct everywhere isolation barracks for the sufferers, to print and distribute five hundred thousand copies of a brochure on the disease, its symptoms and means of cure, to organise on all the streets of the town a special patrol of doctors and their helpers for the giving of first aid to those who had not been removed from private lodgings. It was also decided to run special trains daily on all the railways for the removal of the patients, as the doctors were of the opinion that change of air was one of the best remedies. Similar measures were undertaken at the same time by various associations, societies, and clubs. A "society for struggle with the epidemic" was even founded, and the members gave themselves to the work with remarkable self-devotion. But in spite of all these measures the epidemic gained ground each day, taking in its course old men and little children, working people and resting people, chaste and debauched. And soon the

whole of society was enveloped in the unconquerable elemental terror of the unheard-of calamity.

The flight from Zvezdny commenced. At first only a
few fled, and these were prominent dignitaries, directors,
members of the Legal Chamber and of the Board, who
hastened to send their families to the southern cities of
Australia and Patagonia. Following them, the accidental
elements of the population fled—those foreigners gladly
sojourning in the "gayest city of the southern hemisphere,"
theatrical artists, various business agents, women of light
behaviour. When the epidemic showed no signs of abat-
ing the shopkeepers fled. They hurriedly sold off their
goods and left their empty premises to the will of Fate.
With them went the bankers, the owners of theatres and
restaurants, the editors and the publishers. At last, even
the established inhabitants were moved to go. According
to Law the exit of workmen from the Republic without
special sanction from the Government was forbidden on
pain of loss of pension. Deserters began to increase. The
employés of the town institutions fled, the militia fled,
the hospital nurses fled, the chemists, the doctors. The
desire to flee became in its turn a mania. Everyone fled
who could.

The stations of the electric railway were crushed with
immense crowds, tickets were bought for huge sums of
money and only held by fighting. For a place in a diri-
gible, which took only ten passengers, one paid a whole
fortune. . . . At the moment of the going out of trains,
new people would break into the compartments and
take up places which they would not relinquish except by

compulsion. Crowds stopped the trains which had been fitted up exclusively for patients, dragged the latter out of the carriages and compelled the engine-drivers to go on. From the end of May train service, except between the capital and the ports, ceased to work. From Zvezdny the trains went out overfull, passengers standing on the steps and in the corridors, even daring to cling on outside, despite the fact that with the speed of contemporary electric railways any person doing such a thing risks suffocation. The steamship companies of Australia, South America and South Africa grew inordinately rich, transporting the refugees of the Republic to other lands. The two Southern companies of dirigibles were not less prosperous, accomplishing, as they did, ten journeys a day and bringing away from Zvezdny the last belated millionaires. . . . On the other hand, trains arrived at Zvezdny almost empty; for no wages was it possible to persuade people to come to work at the Capital; only now and again eccentric tourists and seekers of new sensations arrived at the towns. It is reckoned that from the beginning of the exodus to the twenty-second of June, when the regular service of trains ceased, there passed out of Zvezdny by the six railroads some million and a half people, that is, almost two-thirds of the whole population.

By his enterprise, valour, and strength of will, one man earned for himself eternal fame, and that was the President of the Board, Horace Deville. At the special session of the fifth of June, Deville was elected, both by the Board and by the Legal Chamber, Dictator over the town, and was given the title of Nachalnik. He had sole control of the town treasury, of the militia, and of the municipal institutions. At that time it was decided to remove from Zvezdny to a northern port the Government of the Republic and the archives. The name of Horace Deville should be written in letters of gold among the most famous names of history. For six weeks he struggled with the growing anarchy in the town. He succeeded in gathering around him a group of helpers as unselfish as himself. He was able to enforce discipline, both in the militia and in the municipal service generally, for a considerable time, though these bodies were terrified by the general calamity and decimated by the epidemic. Hundreds of thousands owe their escape to Horace Deville, as, thanks to his energy and organising power, it was possible for them to leave. He lightened the misery of the last days of thousands of others, giving them the possibility of dying in hospitals, carefully looked after, and not simply being stoned or beaten to death by the mad crowd. And Deville preserved for mankind the chronicle of the catastrophe, for one cannot but consider as a chronicle his short but pregnant telegrams, sent several times a day from the town of Zvezdny to the temporary residence of the Government of the Republic at the Northern port. Deville's first work on becoming Nachalnik of the town was to attempt to restore calm to the population. He issued manifestos proclaiming that the psychical infection was most quickly caught by people who were excited, and he called upon all healthy and balanced persons to use their authority to restrain the weak and nervous. Then Deville used the Society for Struggle with the Epidemic and put under the authority of its members all public places, theatres, meeting-houses, squares, and streets. In these days there scarcely ever passed an hour but a new case of infection might be discovered. Now here, now there, one saw faces or whole groups of faces manifestly expressive of abnormality. The greater number of the patients, when they understood their condition, showed an immediate desire for help. But under the influence of the disease this wish expressed itself in various types of hostile action directed against these standing near. The stricken wished to hasten home or to a hospital, but instead of doing this they fled in fright to the outskirts of the town. The thought occurred to them to ask the passer-by to do something for them, but instead of that they seized him by the throat. In this way many were suffocated, struck down, or wounded with knife or stick. So the crowd, whenever it found itself in the presence of a man suffering from "contradiction," took to flight. At these moments the members of the Society would appear on the scene, capture the sick man, calm him, and take him to the nearest hospital; it was their work to reason with the crowd and explain that there was really no danger, that the general misfortune had simply spread a little further, and it was their duty to struggle with it to the full extent of their powers.

The sudden infection of persons present in the audience of theatres or meeting-houses often led to the most tragic catastrophes. Once at a performance of opera some hundreds of people stricken mad in a mass, instead of expressing their approval of the vocalists, flung themselves on the stage and scattered blows right and left. At

Valery Bryusov

the Grand Dramatic Theatre, an actor, whose rôle it was to commit suicide by a revolver shot, fired the revolver several times at the public. It was, of course, blank cartridge, but it so acted on the nerves of those present that it hastened the symptoms of the disease in many in whom it was latent. In the confusion which followed several scores of people were killed. But worst of all was that which happened in the Theatre of Fireworks. The detachment of militia posted there in case of fire suddenly set fire to the stage and to the veils by which the various light effects are obtained. Not less than two hundred people were burnt or crushed to death. After that occurrence Horace Deville closed all the theatres and concert-rooms in the town.

The robbers and thieves now began to constitute a grave danger for the inhabitants, and in the general disorganisation they were able to carry their depredations very far. It is said that some of them came to Zvezdny from abroad. Some simulated madness in order to escape punishment, others felt it unnecessary to make any pretence of disguising their open robberies. Gangs of thieves entered the abandoned shops, broke into private lodgings, and took off the more valuable things or demanded gold; they stopped people in the streets and stripped them of their valuables, such as watches, rings, and bracelets. And there accompanied the robberies outrage of every kind, even of the most disgusting. The Nachalnik sent companies of militia to hunt down the criminals, but they did not dare to join in open conflict. There were dreadful moments when among the militia or among the robbers would suddenly appear a case of the disease, and friend would turn his weapon against friend. At first the Nachalnik banished from the town the robbers who fell under arrest. But those who had charge of the prison trains liberated them, in order to take their places. Then the Nachalnik was obliged to condemn the criminals to death. So almost after three centuries' break capital punishment was introduced once more on the earth. In June a general scarcity of the indispensable articles of food and medicine began to make itself felt. The import by rail diminished; manufacture within the town practically ceased. Deville organised the town bakeries and the distribution of bread and meat to the people. In the town itself the same common tables were set up as had long since been established in the factories. But it was not possible to find sufficient people for kitchen and service. Some voluntary workers toiled till they were exhausted, and they gradually diminished in numbers. The town crematoriums flamed all day, but the number of corpses did not decrease but increased. They began to find bodies in the streets and left in houses. The municipal business—such as telegraph, telephone, electric light, water supply, sanitation, and the rest, were worked by fewer and fewer people. It is astonishing how much Deville succeeded in doing. He looked after everything and everyone. One conjectures that he never knew a moment's rest. And all who were saved testify unanimously that his activity was beyond praise.

Towards the middle of June shortage of labour on the railways began to be felt. There were not enough engine-drivers or conductors. On the 17th of July the first accident took place on the South-Western line, the reason being the sudden attack of the engine-driver. In the paroxysm of his disease the driver took his train over a precipice on to a glacier and almost all the passengers were killed or crippled. The news of this was brought to the town by the next train, and it came as a thunderbolt. A hospital train was sent off at once; it brought back the dead and the crippled, but towards the evening of that day news was circulated that a similar catastrophe had taken place on the First line. Two of the railway tracks connecting Zvezdny with the outside world were damaged. Breakdown gangs were sent from Zvezdny and from North Port to repair the lines, but it was almost impossible because of the winter temperature. There was no hope that on these lines train service would be resumed—at least, in the near future.

These catastrophes were simply patterns for new ones. The more alarmed the engine-drivers became the more liable they were to the disease and to the repetition of the mistake of their predecessors. Just because they were afraid of destroying a train they destroyed it. During the five days from the eighteenth to the twenty-second of June seven trains with passengers were wrecked. Thousands of passengers perished from injuries or starved to death unrescued in the snowy wastes. Only very few had sufficient strength to return to the city by their own efforts. The six main lines connecting Zvezdny with the outer world were rendered useless. The service of dirigibles had ceased earlier. One of them had been destroyed by the enraged mob, the pretext given being that they were used exclusively for the rich. The others, one by one, were wrecked, the disease probably attacking the crew. The population of the city was at this time about six hundred thousand. For some time they were only connected with the world by telegraph.

On the 24th of June the Metropolitan railway ceased to run. On the 26th the telephone service was discontinued. On the 27th all chemists' shops, except the large central store, were closed. On the 1st of July the inhabitants were ordered to come from the outer parts of the town into the central districts, so that order might better be maintained, food distributed, and medical aid afforded. Suburban dwellers abandoned their own quarters and settled in those which had lately been abandoned by fugitives. The sense of property vanished. No one was sorry to leave his own, no one felt it strange to take up his abode in other people's houses. Nevertheless, burglars and robbers did not disappear, though perhaps now one would rather call them demented beings than criminals. They continued to steal, and great hoards of gold have been discovered in the empty houses where they hid them, and precious stones beside the decaying body of the robber himself.

It is astonishing that in the midst of universal destruction life tended to keep its former course. There still were shopkeepers who opened their shops and sold for incredible sums the luxuries, flowers, books, guns, and other goods which they had preserved. . . . Purchasers threw down their unnecessary gold ungrudgingly, and miserly merchants hid it, God knows why. There still existed secret resorts, with cards, women, and wine, whither unfortunates sought refuge and tried to forget dreadful reality. There the whole mingled with the diseased, and there is no chronicle of the scenes which took place. Two or three newspapers still tried to preserve the significance of the written word in the midst of desolation. Copies of these newspapers are being sold now at ten or twenty times their original value, and will undoubtedly become bibliographical rarities of the first degree. In their columns is reflected the horrors of the unfortunate town, described in the midst of the reigning madness and set by half-mad compositors. There were reporters who took note of the happenings of the town, journalists who debated hotly the condition of affairs, and even feuilletonists who endeavoured to enliven these tragic days. But the telegrams received from other countries, telling as they did of real healthy life, caused the souls of the readers in Zvezdny to fall into despair.

There were desperate attempts to escape. At the beginning of July an immense crowd of women and children, led by a certain John Dew, decided to set out on foot for the nearest inhabited place, Londontown; Deville understood the madness of this attempt, but could not stop the people, and himself supplied them with warm clothing and provisions. This whole crowd of about two thousand people were lost in the snow and in the continuous Polar night. A certain Whiting started to preach a more heroic remedy: this was, to kill all who were suffering from the disease, and he held that after that the epidemic would cease. He found a considerable number of adherents, though in those dark days the wildest, most inhuman, proposal which in any way promised deliverance would have obtained attention. Whiting and his friends broke into every house in the town and destroyed whatever sick they found. They massacred the patients in the hospitals, they even killed those suspected to be unwell. Robbers and madmen joined themselves to these bands of ideal murderers. The whole town became their arena. In these difficult days Horace Deville organised his fellow-workers into a military force, encouraged them with his spirit, and set out to fight the followers of Whiting. This affair lasted several days. Hundreds of men fell on one side or the other, till at last Whiting himself was taken. He appeared to be in the last stages of *mania contradicens* and had to be taken to the hospital, where he soon perished, instead of to the scaffold.

On the eighth of July one of the worst things happened. The controller of the Central Power Station smashed all the machinery. The electric light failed, and the whole city was plunged into absolute darkness. As there was no other means of lighting and warming the city, the people were left in a helpless plight. Deville had, however, foreseen such an eventuality and had accumulated a considerable quantity of torches and fuel. Bonfires were lighted in all the streets. Torches were distributed in thousands. But these miserable lights could not illumine the gigantic perspectives of the city of Zvezdny, the tens of kilometres of straight line highways, the gloomy height of thirteen-storey buildings. With the darkness the last discipline of the city was lost. Terror and madness finally possessed all souls. The healthy could not be distinguished from the sick. There commenced a dreadful orgy of the despairing.

The moral sense of the people declined with astonishing rapidity. Culture slipped from off these people like a delicate bark, and revealed man, wild and naked, the man-beast as he was. All sense of right was lost, force alone was acknowledged. For women, the only law became that of desire and of indulgence. The most virtuous matrons behaved as the most abandoned, with no continence or faith, and used the vile language of the tavern. Young girls ran about the streets demented and unchaste. Drunkards made feasts in ruined cellars, not in any way distressed that amongst the bottles lay unburied corpses. All this was constantly aggravated by the breaking out of the disease afresh. Sad was the position of children, abandoned by their parents to the will of Fate. They died of hunger, of injury after assault, and they were murdered both purposely and by accident. It is even affirmed that cannibalism took place.

In this last period of tragedy Horace Deville could not, of course, afford help to the whole population. But he did arrange in the Town Hall shelter for those who still preserved their reason. The entrances to the building were barricaded and sentries were kept continuously on guard. There was food and water for three thousand people for forty days. Deville, however, had only eighteen hundred people, and though there must have been other people with sound minds in the town, they could not have known what Deville was doing, and these remained in hiding in the houses. Many resolved to remain indoors till the end, and bodies have been found of many who must have died of hunger in their solitude. It is remarkable that among those who took refuge in the Town Hall there were very few new cases of the disease. Deville was able to keep discipline in his small community. He kept till the last a journal of all that happened, and that journal, together with the telegrams, makes the most reliable source of evidence of the catastrophe. The journal was found in a secret cupboard of the Town Hall, where the most precious documents were kept. The last entry refers to the 20th of July. Deville writes that a demented crowd is assailing the building, and that he is obliged to fire with revolvers upon the people. "What I hope for," he adds, "I know not. No help can be expected before the spring. We have not the food to live till the spring. But I shall fulfil my duty to the end." These were the last words of Deville. Noble words!

It must be added that on the 21st of July the crowd took the Town Hall by storm and its defenders were all killed or scattered. The body of Deville has not yet been found, and there is no reliable evidence as to what took place in the town after the 21st. It must be conjectured, from the state in which the town was found, that anarchy reached its last limits. The gloomy streets, lit up by the glare of bonfires of furniture and books, can be imagined. They obtained fire by striking iron on flint. Crowds of drunkards and madmen danced wildly about the bonfires. Men and women drank together and passed the common cup from lip to lip. The worst scenes of sensuality were witnessed. Some sort of dark atavistic sense enlivened the souls of these townsmen, and half-naked, unwashed, unkempt, they danced the dances of their remote ancestors, the contemporaries of the cave-bears, and they sang the same wild songs as did the hordes when they fell with stone axes upon the mammoth. With songs, with incoherent exclamations, with idiotic laughter, mingled the cries of those who had lost the power to express in words their own delirious dreams, mingled also the moans of those in the convulsions of death. Sometimes dancing gave way to fighting—for a barrel of wine, for a woman, or simply without reason, in a fit of madness brought about by contradictory emotion. There was nowhere to flee; the same dreadful scenes were everywhere, the same orgies everywhere, the same fights, the same brutal gaiety or brutal rage—or else, absolute darkness, which seemed more dreadful, even more intolerable to the staggered imagination.

Zvezdny became an immense black box, in which were some thousands of man-resembling beings, abandoned in the foul air from hundreds of thousands of dead bodies, where amongst the living was not one who understood his own position. This was the city of the senseless, the gigantic madhouse, the greatest and most disgusting Bedlam which the world has ever seen. And the madmen destroyed one another, stabbed or strangled one another, died of madness, died of terror, died of hunger, and of all the diseases which reigned in the infected air.

It goes without saying that the Government of the Republic did not remain indifferent to the great calamity which had overtaken the capital. But it very soon became clear that no help whatever could be given. No doctors, nurses, officers, or workmen of any kind would agree to go to Zvezdny. After the breakdown of the railroad service and of the airships it was, of course, impossible to get there, the climatic conditions being too great an obstacle. Moreover, the attention of the Government was soon absorbed by cases of the disease appearing in other towns of the Republic. In some of these it threatened to take on the same epidemic character, and a social panic set in that was akin to what happened in Zvezdny itself. A wholesale exodus from the more populated parts of the Republic commenced. The work in all the mines came to a standstill, and the entire industrial life of the country faded away. But thanks, however, to strong measures taken in time, the progress of the disease was arrested in these towns, and nowhere did it reach the proportions witnessed in the capital.

The anxiety with which the whole world followed the misfortunes of the young Republic is well known. At first no one dreamed that the trouble could grow to what it did, and the dominant feeling was that of curiosity. The chief newspapers of the world (and in that number our own *Northern European Evening News*) sent their own special correspondents to Zvezdny—to write up the epidemic. Many of these brave knights of the pen became victims of their own professional obligations. When the news became more alarming, various foreign governments and private societies offered their services to the Republic. Some sent troops, others doctors, others money; but the catastrophe developed with such rapidity that this goodwill could not obtain fulfilment. After the breakdown of the railway service the only information received from Zvezdny was that of the telegrams sent by the Nachalnik. These telegrams were forwarded to the ends of the earth and printed in millions of copies. After the wreck of the electrical apparatus the telegraph service lasted still a few days longer, thanks to the accumulators of the power-house. There is no accurate information as to why the telegraph service ceased altogether; perhaps the apparatus was destroyed. The last telegram of Horace Deville was that of the 27th of June. From that date, for almost six weeks, humanity remained without news of the capital of the Republic.

During July several attempts were made to reach Zvezdny by air. Several new airships and aeroplanes were received by the Republic. But for a long time all efforts to reach the city failed. At last, however, the aeronaut, Thomas Billy, succeeded in flying to the unhappy town. He picked up from the roof of the town two people in an extreme state of hunger and mental collapse. Looking through the ventilators Billy saw that the streets were plunged in absolute darkness; but he heard wild cries, and understood that there were still living human beings in the town. Billy, however, did not dare to let himself down into the town itself. Towards the end of August one line of the electric railway was put in order as far as the station Lissis, a hundred and five kilometres from the town. A detachment of well-armed men passed into the town, bearing food and medical first-aid, entering by the north-western gates. They, however, could not penetrate further than the first blocks of buildings, because of the dreadful atmosphere. They had to do their work step by step, clearing the bodies from the streets, disinfecting the air as they went. The only people whom they met were completely irresponsible. They resembled wild animals in their ferocity and had to be captured and held by force. About the middle of September train service with Zvezdny was once more established and trains went regularly.

At the time of writing the greater part of the town has already been cleared. Electric light and heating are once more in working order. The only part of the town which has not been dealt with is the American quarter, but it is thought that there are no living beings there. About ten thousand people have been saved, but the greater number are apparently incurable. Those who have to any degree recovered evince a strong disinclination to speak of the life they have gone through. What is more, their stories are full of contradiction and often not confirmed by documentary evidence. Various newspapers of the last days of July have been found. The latest to date, that of the 22nd of July, gives the news of the death of Horace Deville and the invitation of shelter in the Town Hall. There are, indeed, some other pages marked August, but the words printed thereon make it clear that the author (who was probably setting in type his own delirium) was quite irresponsible. The diary of Horace Deville was discovered, with its regular chronicle of events from the 28th of June to the 20th of July. The frenzies of the last days in the town are luridly witnessed by the things discovered in streets and houses. Mutilated bodies everywhere: the bodies of the starved, of the suffocated, of those murdered by the insane, and some even half-eaten. Bodies were found in the most unexpected places: in the tunnels of the Metropolitan railway, in sewers, in various sheds, in boilers. The demented had sought refuge from the surrounding terrors in all possible places. The interiors of most houses had been wrecked, and the booty which robbers had found it impossible to dispose of had been hidden in secret rooms and cellars.

It will certainly be several months before Zvezdny will become habitable once more. Now it is almost empty. The town, which could accommodate three million people, has but thirty thousand workmen, who are cleansing the streets and houses. A good number of the former inhabitants who had previously fled have returned, however, to seek the bodies of their relatives and to glean the remains of their lost fortunes. Several tourists, attracted by the amazing spectacle of the empty town, have also arrived. Two business men have opened hotels and are doing pretty well. A small café-chantant is to be opened shortly, the troupe for which has already been engaged.

The Northern European Evening News has for its part sent out a new correspondent, Mr. Andrew Ewald, and hopes to obtain circumstantial news of all the fresh discoveries which may be made in the unfortunate capital of the Republic of the Southern Cross.

1907

THE THIRD DRUG

E. Nesbit

I.

Roger Wroxham looked round his studio before he blew out the candle, and wondered whether, perhaps, he looked for the last time. It was large and empty, yet his trouble had filled it and, pressing against him in the prison of those four walls, forced him out into the world, where lights and voices and the presence of other men should give him room to draw back, to set a space between it and him, to decide whether he would ever face it again—he and it alone together. The nature of his trouble is not germane to this story. There was a woman in it, of course, and money, and a friend, and regrets and embarrassments—and all of these reached out tendrils that wove and interwove till they made a puzzle problem of which heart and brain were now weary.

He blew out the candle and went quietly downstairs. It was nine at night, a soft night of May in Paris. Where should he go? He thought of the Seine, and took—an omnibus. When at last it stopped he got off, and so strange was the place to him that it almost seemed as though the trouble itself had been left behind. He did not feel it in the length of three or four streets that he traversed slowly. But in the open space, very light and lively, where he recognised the Taverne de Paris and knew himself in Montmartre, the trouble set its teeth in his heart again, and he broke away from the lamps and the talk to struggle with it in the dark, quiet streets beyond.

A man braced for such a fight has little thought to spare for the details of his surroundings. The next thing that Wroxham knew of the outside world was the fact which he had known for some time that he was not alone in the street. There was someone on the other side of the road keeping pace with him—yes, certainly keeping pace, for, as he slackened his own, the feet on the other pavement also went more slowly. And now they were four feet, not two. Where had the other man sprung from? He had not been there a moment ago. And now, from an archway a little ahead of him, a third man came.

Wroxham stopped. Then three men converged upon him, and, like a sudden magic-lantern picture on a sheet prepared, there came to him all that he had heard and read of Montmartre—dark archways, knives, Apaches, and men who went away from homes where they were beloved and never again returned. He, too—well, if he never returned again, it would be quicker than the Seine, and, in the event of ultramundane possibilities, safer.

He stood still and laughed in the face of the man who first reached him.

"Well, my friend?" said he; and at that the other two drew close.

"Monsieur walks late," said the first, a little confused, as it seemed, by that laugh.

"And will walk still later if it pleases him," said Roger. "Good night, my friends."

"Ah!" said the second, "friends do not say adieu so quickly. Monsieur will tell us the hour."

"I have not a watch," said Roger, quite truthfully.

"I will assist you to search for it," said the third man, and laid a hand on his arm.

Roger threw it off. The man with the hand staggered back.

"The knife searches more surely," said the second.

"No, no," said the third, quickly; "he is too heavy. I for one will not carry him afterwards."

They closed round him, hustling him between them. Their pale, degenerate faces spun and swung round him in the struggle. For there was a struggle. He had not meant that there should be a struggle. Someone would hear—someone would come.

But if any heard none came. The street retained its empty silence; the houses, masked in close shutters, kept their reserve. The four were wrestling, all pressed close together in a writhing bunch, drawing breath hardly through set teeth, their feet slipping and not slipping on the rounded cobble-stones.

The contact with these creatures, the smell of them, and the warm, greasy texture of their flesh as, in the conflict, his face or neck met neck or face of theirs—Roger felt a cold rage possess him. He wrung two clammy hands apart and threw something off—something that staggered back clattering, fell in the gutter, and lay there.

It was then that Roger felt the knife. Its point glanced off the cigarette-case in his breast pocket and bit sharply at his inner arm. And at the sting of it Roger knew, suddenly and quite surely, that he did not desire to die. He feigned a reeling weakness, relaxed his grip, swayed sideways, and then suddenly caught the other two in a new grip, crushed their faces together, flung them off, and ran. It was but for an instant that his feet were the only ones that echoed in the street. Then he knew that the others too were running.

It was like one of those nightmares wherein one runs for ever, leaden-footed, through a city of the dead. Roger turned sharply to the right. The sound of the other footsteps told that the pursuers also had turned that corner. Here was another street—a steep ascent. He ran more swiftly—he was running now for his life—the life that he held so cheap three minutes before. And all the streets were empty—empty like dream-streets, with all their windows dark and unhelpful, their doors fast closed against his need. Only now and again he glanced to right or left, if perchance some window might show light to justify a cry for help, some door advance the welcome of an open inch.

There was at last such a door. He did not see it till it was almost behind him. Then there was the drag of the sudden stop—the eternal instant of indecision. Was there time? There must be. He dashed his fingers through the inch-crack, grazing the backs of them, leapt within, drew the door outside; there was the sound of feet that went away.

He found himself listening, listening, and there was nothing to hear but the silence, and once, before he thought to twist his handkerchief round it, the drip of blood from his hand.

By and by he knew that he was not alone in this house, for from far away there came the faint sound of a footstep, and, quite near, the faint answering echo of it. And at a window high up on the other side of the courtyard a light showed. Light and sound and echo intensified, the light passing window after window, till at last it moved across the courtyard and the little trees threw black shifting shadows as it came towards him—a lamp in the hand of a man.

It was a short, bald man, with pointed beard and bright, friendly eyes. He held the lamp high as he came, and when he saw Roger he drew his breath in an inspiration that spoke of surprise, sympathy, pity.

"Hold! Hold!" He said, in a singularly pleasant voice; "there has been a misfortune? You are wounded, monsieur?"

"Apaches," said Roger, and was surprised at the weakness of his own voice.

"Your hand?"

"My arm," said Roger.

"Fortunately," said the other, "I am a surgeon. Allow me."

He set the lamp on the step of a closed door, took off Roger's coat, and quickly tied his own handkerchief round the wounded arm.

"Now," he said, "courage! I am alone in the house. No one comes here but me. If you can walk up to my rooms you will save us both much trouble. If you cannot, sit here and I will fetch you a cordial. But I advise you to try to walk. That *port cochère* is, unfortunately, not very strong, and the lock is a common spring lock, and your friends may return with *their* friends; whereas the door across the courtyard is heavy, and the bolts are new."

Roger moved towards the heavy door whose bolts were new. The stairs seemed to go on forever. The doctor lent his arm, but the carved banisters and their lively shadows whirled before Roger's eyes. Also he seemed to be shod with lead, and to have in his legs bones that were red hot. Then the stairs ceased, and there was light, and a cessation of the dragging of those leaden feet. He was on a couch, and his eyes might close.

When next he saw and heard he was lying at ease, the close intimacy of a bandage clasping his arm, and in his mouth the vivid taste of some cordial.

The doctor was sitting in an armchair near a table, looking benevolent through gold-rimmed pince-nez.

"Better?" He said. "No; lie still, you'll be a new man soon."

"I am desolated," said Roger, "to have occasioned you all this trouble."

"Not at all," said the doctor. "We live to heal, and it is a nasty cut, that in your arm. If you are wise, you will rest at present. I shall be honoured if you will be my guest for the night."

Roger again murmured something about trouble.

"In a big house like this," said the doctor, as it seemed a little sadly, "there are many empty rooms, and some rooms which are not empty. There is a bed altogether at your service, monsieur, and I counsel you not to delay in seeking it. You can walk?"

Wroxham stood up. "Why, yes," he said, stretching himself. "I feel, as you say, a new man."

A narrow bed and rush-bottomed chair showed like doll's-house furniture in the large, high, gaunt room to which the doctor led him.

"You are too tired to undress yourself," said the doctor; "rest—only rest," and covered him with a rug, snugly tucked him up, and left him.

"I leave the door open," he said, "in case you should have any fever. Good night. Do not torment yourself. All goes well."

Then he took away the lamp, and Wroxham lay on his back and saw the shadows of the window-frames cast by the street lamps on the high ceiling. His eyes, growing accustomed to the darkness, perceived the carving of the white paneled walls and mantelpiece. There was a door in the room, another door than the one which the doctor had left open. Roger did not like open doors. The other door, however, was closed. He wondered where it led, and whether it were locked. Presently he got up to see. It was locked. He lay down again.

His arm gave him no pain, and the night's adventure did not seem to have over set his nerves. He felt, on the contrary, calm, confident, extraordinarily at ease, and master of himself. The trouble—how could that ever have seemed important? This calmness—it felt like the calmness that precedes sleep. Yet sleep was far from him. What was it that kept sleep away? The bed was comfortable— the pillows soft. What was it? It came to him presently that it was the scent which distracted him, worrying him with a memory that he could not define. A faint scent of—what was it? Perfumery? Yes—and camphor—and something else—something vaguely disquieting. He had not noticed it before he had risen and tried the handle of that other door. But now——He covered his face with the sheet, but through the sheet he smelt it still. He rose and threw back one of the long French windows. It opened with a click and a jar, and he looked across the dark well of the courtyard. He leaned out, breathing the chill pure air of the May night, but when he withdrew his head the scent was there again. Camphor—perfume—and something else. What was it that it reminded him of? He had his knee on the bed-edge when the answer came to that question. It was the scent that had struck at him from the darkened room when, a child, clutching at a grown-up hand, he had been led to the bed where, amid flowers, something white lay under a sheet—his mother they had told him. It was the scent of death, disguised with drugs and perfumes.

He stood up and went, with carefully controlled swiftness, towards the open door. He wanted light and a human voice. The doctor was in the room upstairs; he——

The doctor was face to face with him on the landing, not a yard away, moving towards him quietly in shoeless feet.

"I can't sleep," said Wroxham, a little wildly; "it's too dark and——"

"Come upstairs," said the doctor, and Wroxham went.

There was comfort in the large, lighted room. A green shaded lamp stood on the table.

"What's behind that door," said Wroxham, abruptly—"that door downstairs?"

"Specimens," the doctor answered; "preserved specimens. My line is physiological research. You understand?"

So that was it.

"I feel quite well, you know," said Wroxham, laboriously explaining—"fit as any man—only I can't sleep."

"I see," said the doctor.

"It's the scent from your specimens, I think," Wroxham went on; "there's something about that scent."

"Yes," said the doctor.

"It's very odd." Wroxham was leaning his elbow on his knee and his chin on his hand. "I feel so frightfully well——and yet there's a strange feeling——"

"Yes," said the doctor. "Yes, tell me exactly how you feel."

"I feel," said Wroxham, slowly, "like a man on the crest of a wave."

The doctor stood up.

"You feel well, happy, full of life and energy—as though you could walk to the world's end, and yet——"

"And yet," said Roger, "as though my next step might be my last—as though I might step into a grave."

He shuddered.

"Do you," asked the doctor, anxiously—"do you feel thrills of pleasure—something like the first waves of chloroform—thrills running from your hair to your feet?"

"I felt all that," said Roger, slowly, "downstairs before I opened the window."

The doctor looked at his watch, frowned, and got up quickly. "There is very little time," he said.

Suddenly Roger felt an unexplained thrill of pain.

The doctor went to a long laboratory bench with bottle-filled shelves above it, and on it crucibles and retorts, test tubes, beakers—all a chemist's apparatus—reached a bottle from a shelf, and measured out certain drops into a graduated glass, added water, and stirred it with a glass rod.

"Drink that," he said.

"No," said Roger, and as he spoke a thrill like the first thrill of the first chloroform wave swept through him, and it was a thrill, not of pleasure, but of pain. "No," he said, and "Ah!" for the pain was sharp.

"If you don't drink," said the doctor carefully, "you are a dead man."

"You may be giving me poison," Roger gasped, his hands at his heart.

"I may," said the doctor. "What do you suppose poison makes you feel like? What do you feel like now?"

"I feel," said Roger, "like death."

Every nerve, every muscle thrilled to a pain not too intense to be underlined by a shuddering nausea. "Like death," he said again.

"Then drink," cried the doctor, in tones of such cordial entreaty, such evident anxiety, that Wroxham half held his hand out for the glass. "Drink! Believe me, it is your only chance."

Again the pain swept through him like an electric current. The beads of sweat sprang out on his forehead.

"That wound," the doctor pleaded, standing over him with the glass held out. "For Heaven's sake, drink! Don't you understand, man? You *are* poisoned. Your wound——"

"The knife?" Wroxham murmured, and as he spoke his eyes seemed to swell in his head, and his head itself to grow enormous. "Do you know the poison—and its antidote?"

"I know all," the doctor soothed him. "Drink, then, my friend."

As the pain caught him again in a clasp more close than any lover's he clutched at the glass and drank. The drug met the pain and mastered it. Roger, in the ecstasy of pain's cessation, saw the world fade and go out in a haze of vivid violet.

II.

Faint films of lassitude shot with contentment wrapped him round. He lay passive as a man lies in the convalescence that follows a long fight with Death.

"I'm better now," he said, in a voice that was a whisper— tried to raise his hand from where it lay helpless in his sight, failed, and lay looking at it in confident repose— "much better."

"Yes," said the doctor, and his pleasant, soft voice had grown softer, pleasanter. "You are now in the second stage. An interval is necessary before you can pass to the third. I will enliven the interval by conversation. Is there anything you would like to know?"

"Nothing," said Roger; "I am quite happy—quite contented."

"This is very interesting," said the doctor. "Tell me exactly how you feel."

Roger faintly and slowly told him.

"Ah!" the doctor said, "I have not before heard this. You are the only one of them all who ever passed the first stage. The others——"

"The others?" said Roger, but he did not care much about the others.

"The others," said the doctor, frowning, "were unsound. Decadent students, degenerate Apaches. You are highly trained—in fine physical condition. And your brain! The Lord be good to the Apaches who so delicately excited it to just the degree of activity needed for my purpose."

"The others?" Wroxham insisted.

"The others? They are in the room whose door was locked. Look—you should be able to see them. The second drug should lay your consciousness before me like a sheet of white paper on which I can write what I choose. If I choose that you should see my specimens——*Allons donc*. I have no secrets from you now. Look, look—strain your eyes. In theory, I know all that you can do and feel and see in this second stage. But practically——Enlighten me—look—shut your eyes and look!"

Roger closed his eyes and looked. He saw the gaunt, uncarpeted staircase, the open doors of the big rooms, passed to the locked door, and it opened at his touch. The room inside was, like the other, spacious and paneled. A lighted lamp with a blue shade hung from the ceiling, and below it an effect of spread whiteness. Roger looked. There *were* things to be seen.

With a shudder he opened his eyes on the doctor's delightful room, the doctor's intent face.

"What did you see?" the doctor asked. "Tell me!"

"Did you kill them all?" Roger asked back.

"They died—of their own inherent weakness," the doctor said. "And you saw them?"

"I saw," said Roger, "the quiet people lying all along the floor in their death clothes—the people who have come in at that door of yours that is a trap—for robbery, or curiosity, or shelter—and never gone out any more."

"Right," said the doctor. "Right. My theory is proved at every point. You can see what I choose you to see. Yes; decadents all. It was in embalming that I was a specialist before I began these other investigations."

"What," Roger whispered—"what is it all for?"

"To make the superman," said the doctor. "I will tell you."

He told. It was a long story—the story of a man's life, a man's work, a man's dreams, hopes, ambitions.

"The secret of life," the doctor ended. "That is what all the alchemists sought. They sought it where Fate pleased. I sought it where I have found it—in death."

Roger thought of the room behind the locked door.

"And the secret is?" asked Roger.

"I have told you," said the doctor, impatiently; "it is in the third drug that life—splendid, superhuman life—is found. I have tried it on animals. Always they became perfect, all that an animal should be. And more, too—much more. They were too perfect, too near humanity. They looked at me with human eyes. I could not let them live. Such animals it is not necessary to embalm. I had a laboratory in those days—and assistants. They called me the Prince of Vivisectors."

The man on the sofa shuddered.

"I am naturally," the doctor went on, "a tender-hearted man. You see it in my face; my voice proclaims it. Think what I have suffered in the sufferings of these poor beasts who never injured me. May God bear witness that I have not buried my talent. I have been faithful. I have laid it down all—love, and joy, and pity, and the little beautiful things of life—all, all, on the altar of science, and seen them consume away. I deserve my heaven, if ever man did. And now by all the saints in heaven I am near it!"

"What is the third drug?" Roger asked, lying limp and flat on his couch.

"It is the Elixir of Life," said the doctor. "I am not its discoverer; the old alchemists knew it well, but they failed because they sought to apply the elixir to a normal—that is, a diseased and faulty—body. I knew better. One must have first a body abnormally healthy, abnormally strong. Then, not the elixir, but the two drugs that prepare. The first excites prematurely the natural conflict between the principles of life and death, and then, just at the point where Death is about to win his victory, the second drug intensifies life so that it conquers—intensifies, and yet chastens. Then the whole life of the subject, risen to an ecstasy, falls prone in an almost voluntary submission to the coming super-life. Submission—submission! The garrison must surrender before the splendid conqueror can enter and make the citadel his own. Do you understand? Do you submit?"

"I submit," said Roger, for, indeed, he did. "But—soon—quite soon—I will not submit."

He was too weak to be wise, or those words had remained unspoken.

The doctor sprang to his feet.

"It works too quickly!" he cried. "Everything works too quickly with you. Your condition is too perfect. So now I bind you."

From a drawer beneath the bench where the bottles gleamed, the doctor drew rolls of bandages—violet, like the haze that had drowned, at the urgence of the second drug, the consciousness of Roger. He moved, faintly resistant, on his couch. The doctor's hands, most gently, most irresistibly, controlled his movement.

"Lie still," said the gentle, charming voice. "Lie still; all is well." The clever, soft hands were unrolling the bandages—passing them round arms and throat—under and over the soft narrow couch. "I cannot risk your life, my poor boy. The least movement of yours might ruin everything. The third drug, like the first, must be offered directly to the blood which absorbs it. I bound the first drug as an unguent upon your knife-wound."

The swift hands passed the soft bandages back and forth, over and under—flashes of violet passed to and fro in the air like the shuttle of a weaver through his warp. As the bandage clasped his knees Roger moved.

"For God's sake, no!" the doctor cried; "the time is so near. If you cease to submit it is death."

With an incredible accelerated swiftness he swept the bandages round and round knees and ankles, drew a deep breath—stood upright.

"I must make an incision," he said—"in the head this time. It will not hurt. See! I spray it with the Constantia Nepenthe; that also I discovered. My boy, in a moment you know all things—you are as a god. Be patient. Preserve your submission."

And Roger, with life and will resurgent hammering at his heart, preserved it.

He did not feel the knife that made the cross cut on his temple, but he felt the hot spurt of blood that followed the cut, he felt the cool flap of a plaster spread with some sweet, clean smelling unguent that met the blood and stanched it. There was a moment—or was it hours?—of nothingness. Then from that cut on his forehead there seemed to radiate threads of infinite length, and of a strength that one could trust to—threads that linked one to all knowledge past and present. He felt that he controlled all wisdom, as a driver controls his four-in-hand. Knowledge, he perceived, belonged to him as the air belongs to the eagle. He swam in it, as a great fish in a limitless ocean.

He opened his eyes and met those of the doctor, who sighed as one to whom breath has grown difficult.

"Ah, all goes well. Oh, my boy, was it not worth it? What do you feel?"

"I. Know. Everything," said Roger, with full stops between the words.

"Everything? The future?"

"No. I know all that man has ever known."

"Look back—into the past. See someone. See Pharaoh. You see him—on his throne?"

"Not on his throne. He is whispering in a corner of his great gardens to a girl who is the daughter of a water-carrier."

"Bah! Any poet of my dozen decadents who lie so still could have told me that. Tell me secrets—the *Masque de Fer*."

The other told a tale, wild and incredible, but it satisfied the listener.

"That too—it might be imagination. Tell me the name of the woman I loved and—"

The echo of the name of the anesthetic came to Roger; "Constantia," said he, in an even voice.

"Ah," the doctor cried, "now I see you know all things. It was not murder. I hoped to dower her with all the splendors of the superlife."

"Her bones lie under the lilacs, where you used to kiss her in the spring," said Roger, quite without knowing what it was that he was going to say.

"It is enough," the doctor cried. He sprang up, arranged certain bottles and glasses on a table convenient to his chair. "You know all things. It was not a dream, this, the dream of my life. It is true. It is a fact accomplished. Now I, too, will know all things. I will be as the gods."

He sought among leather cases on a far table and came back swiftly into the circle of light that lay below the green-shaded lamp.

Roger, floating contentedly on the new sea of knowledge that seemed to support him, turned eyes on the trouble that had driven him out of that large, empty studio so long ago, so far away. His new-found wisdom laughed at that problem, laughed and solved it. "To end that trouble I must do so-and-so, say such-and-such," Roger told himself again and again.

And now the doctor, standing by the table, laid on it his pale, plump hand outspread. He drew a knife from a case—a long, shiny knife—and scored his hand across and across its back, as a cook scores pork for cooking. The slow blood followed the cuts in beads and lines.

Into the cuts he dropped a green liquid from a little bottle, replaced its stopper, bound up his hand, and sat down.

"The beginning of the first stage," he said; "almost at once I shall begin to be a new man. It will work quickly. My body, like yours, is sane and healthy."

There was a long silence.

"Oh, but this is good," the doctor broke it to say. "I feel the hand of Life sweeping my nerves like harp-strings."

Roger had been thinking, the old common sense that guides an ordinary man breaking through this consciousness of illimitable wisdom. "You had better," he said, "unbind me; when the hand of Death sweeps your nerves you may need help."

"No," the doctor said, and no, and no, and no many times. "I am afraid of you. You know all things, and even in your body you are stronger than I."

And then suddenly and irresistibly the pain caught him. Roger saw his face contorted with agony, his hands clenching on the arm of his chair; and it seemed that either this man was less able to bear pain than he, or that the pain was much more violent than had been his own. And the plump, pale hand, writhing and distorted by anguish, again and again drew near to take the glass that stood ready on the table, and with convulsive self-restraint again and again drew back without it.

The short May night was waning—the shiver of dawn rustled the leaves of the plant whose leaves were like red misshaped hearts.

"Now!" The doctor screamed the word, grasped the glass, drained it, and sank back in his chair. His hand struck the table beside him. Looking at his limp body and head thrown back one could almost see the cessation of pain, the coming of kind oblivion.

III.

The dawn had grown to daylight, a poor, grey, rain-stained daylight, not strong enough to pierce the curtains and persiennes, and yet not so weak but that it could mock the lamp, now burnt low and smelling vilely.

Roger lay very still on his couch, a man wounded, anxious, and extravagantly tired. In those hours of long, slow dawning, face to face with the unconscious figure in the chair, he had felt, slowly and little by little, the recession of that sea of knowledge on which he had felt himself float in such large content. The sea had withdrawn itself, leaving him high and dry on the shore of the normal. The only relic that he had clung to and that he still grasped was the answer to the problem of the trouble—the only wisdom that he had put into words. These words remained to him, and he knew that they held wisdom—very simple wisdom, too.

"To end the trouble I must do so-and-so and say such-and-such."

Slowly a dampness spread itself over Wroxham's forehead and tingled among the roots of his hair. He writhed in his bonds. They held fast. He could not move hand or foot. Only his head could turn a little, so that he could at will see the doctor or not see him. A shaft of desolate light pierced the persienne at its hinge and rested on the table, where an overturned glass lay.

Wroxham thrilled from head to foot. The body in the chair stirred—hardly stirred—shivered, rather—and a very faint, far-away voice said:—

"Now the third—give me the third."

"What?" said Roger, stupidly; and he had to clear his throat twice before he could say even that.

"The moment is now," said the doctor. "I remember all. I made you a god. Give me the third drug."

"Where is it?" Roger asked.

"It is at my elbow," the doctor murmured. "I submit—I submit. Give me the third drug, and let me be as you are."

"As *I* am?" said Roger. "You forget. *I* am bound."

"Break your bonds," the doctor urged, in a quick, small voice. "I trust you now. You are stronger than all men, as you are wiser. Stretch your muscles, and the bandages will fall asunder like snow-wreaths."

"It is too late," Wroxham said, and laughed; "all that is over. I am not wise any more, and I have only the strength of a man. I am tired and wounded. I cannot break my bonds—I cannot help you!"

"But if you cannot help me—it is death," said the doctor.

E. Nesbit

"It is death," said Roger. "Do you feel it coming on you?"

"I feel life returning," said the doctor, "it is now the moment—the one possible moment. And I cannot reach it. Oh, give it me—give it me!"

Then Roger cried out suddenly, in a loud voice: "Now, by all that's sacred, you infernal decadent, I am *glad* that I cannot give it. Yes, if it costs me my life, it's worth it, you madman, so that your life ends too. Now be silent, and die like a man if you have it in you."

Roger lay and watched him, and presently he writhed from the chair to the floor, tearing feebly at it with his fingers, moaned, shuddered, and lay very still.

Of all that befell Roger in that house the worst was now. For now he knew that he was alone with the dead, and between him and death stretched certain hours and days. For the *porte cochère* was locked; the doors of the house itself were locked—heavy doors and the locks new.

"I am alone in the house," the doctor had said. "No one comes here but me."

No one would come. He would die there—he, Roger Wroxham—"poor old Roger Wroxham, who was no one's enemy but his own." Tears pricked his eyes. He shook his head impatiently and they fell from his lashes.

"You fool," he said, "can't *you* die like a man either?"

Then he set his teeth and made himself lie still. It seemed to him that now Despair laid her hand on his heart. But, to speak truth, it was Hope whose hand lay there. This was so much more than a man should be called on to bear—it could not be true. It was an evil dream. He would awake presently. Or if it were, indeed, real—then someone would come, someone must come. God could not let nobody come to save him.

And late at night, when heart and brain had been stretched almost to the point where both break and let in the sea of madness, someone came.

The interminable day had worn itself out. Roger had screamed, yelled, shouted till his throat was dried up, his lips baked and cracked. No one heard. How should they? The twilight had thickened and thickened till at last it made a shroud for the dead man on the floor by the chair. And there were other dead men in that house; and as Roger ceased to see the one he saw the others—the quiet, awful faces, the lean hands, the straight, stiff limbs laid out one beyond another in the room of death. They at least were not bound. If they should rise in their white wrappings and, crossing that empty sleeping chamber very softly, come slowly up the stairs——

A stair creaked.

His ears, strained with hours of listening, thought themselves befooled. But his cowering heart knew better.

Again a stair creaked. There was a hand on the door.

"Then it is all over," said Roger in the darkness, "and I *am* mad."

The door opened very slowly, very cautiously. There was no light. Only the sound of soft feet and draperies that rustled. Then suddenly a match spurted—light struck at his eyes; a flicker of lit candlewick steadying to flame. And the things that had come were not those quiet people creeping up to match their death with his death in life, but human creatures, alive, breathing, with eyes that moved and glittered, lips that breathed and spoke.

"He must be here," one said. "Lisette watched all day; he never came out. He must be here—there is nowhere else."

Then they set up the candle-end on the table, and he saw their faces. They were the Apaches who had set on him in that lonely street, and who had sought him here—to set on him again.

He sucked his dry tongue, licked his dry lips, and cried aloud:—

"Here I am! Oh, kill me! For the love of Heaven, brothers, kill me *now*!"

And even before he spoke they had seen him, and seen what lay on the floor.

"He died this morning. I am bound. Kill me, brothers; I cannot die slowly here alone. Oh, kill me, for pity's sake!"

But already the three were pressing on each other at a doorway suddenly grown too narrow. They could kill a living man, but they could not face death, quiet, enthroned.

"For the love of Heaven," Roger screamed, "have pity! Kill me outright! Come back—come back!"

And then, since even Apaches are human, they did come back. One of them caught up the candle and bent over Roger, knife in hand.

"Make sure!" said Roger, through set teeth.

"*Nom d'un nom*," said the Apache, with worse words, and cut the bandages here, and here, and here again, and there, and lower, to the very feet.

Then this good Samaritan helped Roger to rise, and when he could not stand, the Samaritan half pulled, half carried him down those many steps, till they came upon the others putting on their boots at the stair-foot.

Then between them the three men carried the other out and slammed the outer door, and presently set him against a gate-post in another street, and went their wicked ways.

And after a time a girl with furtive eyes brought brandy and hoarse muttered kindnesses, and slid away in the shadows.

Against that gate-post the police came upon him. They took him to the address they found on him. When they came to question him he said, "Apaches," and his variations on that theme were deemed sufficient, though not one of them touched truth or spoke of the third drug.

There has never been anything in the papers about that house. I think it is still closed, and inside it still lie in the locked room the very quiet people; and above, there is the room with the narrow couch and the scattered, cut, violet bandages, and the Thing on the floor by the chair, under the lamp that burned itself out in that May dawning.

1908

A VICTIM OF HIGHER SPACE

Algernon Blackwood

"There's a hextraordinary gentleman to see you, sir," said the new man.

"Why 'extraordinary'?" asked Dr. Silence, drawing the tips of his thin fingers through his brown beard. His eyes twinkled pleasantly. "Why 'extraordinary,' Barker?" he repeated encouragingly, noticing the perplexed expression in the man's eyes.

"He's so—so thin, sir. I could hardly see 'im at all—at first. He was inside the house before I could ask the name," he added, remembering strict orders.

"And who brought him here?"

"He come alone, sir, in a closed cab. He pushed by me before I could say a word—making no noise, not what I could hear. He seemed to move so soft like—"

The man stopped short with obvious embarrassment, as though he had already said enough to jeopardise his new situation, but trying hard to show that he remembered the instructions and warnings he had received with regard to the admission of strangers not properly accredited.

"And where is the gentleman now?" asked Dr. Silence, turning away to conceal his amusement.

"I really couldn't exactly say, sir. I left him standing in the 'all—"

The doctor looked up sharply. "But why in the hall, Barker? Why not in the waiting-room?" He fixed his piercing though kindly eyes on the man's face. "Did he frighten you?" he asked quickly.

"I think he did, sir, if I may say so. I seemed to lose sight of him, as it were—" The man stammered, evidently convinced by now that he had earned his dismissal. "He come in so funny, just like a cold wind," he added boldly, setting his heels at attention and looking his master full in the face.

The doctor made an internal note of the man's halting description; he was pleased that the slight signs of psychic intuition which had induced him to engage Barker had not entirely failed at the first trial. Dr. Silence sought this qualification in all his assistants, from secretary to serving man, and if it surrounded him with a somewhat singular crew, the drawbacks were more than compensated for on the whole by their occasional flashes of insight.

"So the gentleman made you feel queer, did he?"

"That was it, I think, sir," repeated the man stolidly.

"And he brings no kind of introduction to me—no letter or anything?" asked the doctor, with feigned surprise, as though he knew what was coming.

The man fumbled, both in mind and pockets, and finally produced an envelope.

"I beg pardon, sir," he said, greatly flustered; "the gentleman handed me this for you."

It was a note from a discerning friend, who had never yet sent him a case that was not vitally interesting from one point or another.

"Please see the bearer of this note," the brief message ran, "though I doubt if even you can do much to help him."

John Silence paused a moment, so as to gather from the mind of the writer all that lay behind the brief words of the letter. Then he looked up at his servant with a graver expression than he had yet worn.

"Go back and find this gentleman," he said, "and show him into the green study. Do not reply to his question, or speak more than actually necessary; but think kind, helpful, sympathetic thoughts as strongly as you can, Barker. You remember what I told you about the importance of *thinking*, when I engaged you. Put curiosity out of your mind, and think gently, sympathetically, affectionately, if you can."

He smiled, and Barker, who had recovered his composure in the doctor's presence, bowed silently and went out.

There were two different reception-rooms in Dr. Silence's house. One (intended for persons who imagined they needed spiritual assistance when really they were only candidates for the asylum) had padded walls, and was well supplied with various concealed contrivances by means of which sudden violence could be instantly met and overcome. It was, however, rarely used. The other, intended for the reception of genuine cases of spiritual distress and out-of-the-way afflictions of a psychic nature, was entirely draped and furnished in a soothing deep green, calculated to induce calmness and repose of mind. And this room was the one in which Dr. Silence interviewed the majority of his "queer" cases, and the one into which he had directed Barker to show his present caller.

To begin with, the arm-chair in which the patient was always directed to sit, was nailed to the floor, since its immovability tended to impart this same excellent characteristic to the occupant. Patients invariably grew excited when talking about themselves, and their excitement tended to confuse their thoughts and to exaggerate their language. The inflexibility of the chair helped to counteract this. After repeated endeavours to drag it forward, or push it back, they ended by resigning themselves to sitting quietly. And with the futility of fidgeting there followed a calmer state of mind.

Upon the floor, and at intervals in the wall immediately behind, were certain tiny green buttons, practically unnoticeable, which on being pressed permitted a soothing and persuasive narcotic to rise invisibly about the occupant of the chair. The effect upon the excitable patient was rapid, admirable, and harmless. The green study was further provided with a secret spy-hole; for John Silence liked when possible to observe his patient's face before it had assumed that mask the features of the human countenance invariably wear in the presence of another person. A man sitting alone wears a psychic expression; and this expression is the man himself. It disappears the moment another person joins him. And Dr. Silence often learned more from a few moments' secret observation of a face than from hours of conversation with its owner afterwards.

A very light, almost a dancing step followed Barker's heavy tread towards the green room, and a moment afterwards the man came in and announced that the

Algernon Blackwood

gentleman was waiting. He was still pale and his manner nervous.

"Never mind, Barker" the doctor said kindly; "if you were not psychic the man would have had no effect upon you at all. You only need training and development. And when you have learned to interpret these feelings and sensations better, you will feel no fear, but only a great sympathy."

"Yes, sir; thank you, sir!" And Barker bowed and made his escape, while Dr. Silence, an amused smile lurking about the corners of his mouth, made his way noiselessly down the passage and put his eye to the spy-hole in the door of the green study.

This spy-hole was so placed that it commanded a view of almost the entire room, and, looking through it, the doctor saw a hat, gloves, and umbrella lying on a chair by the table, but searched at first in vain for their owner.

The windows were both closed and a brisk fire burned in the grate. There were various signs—signs intelligible at least to a keenly intuitive soul—that the room was occupied, yet so far as human beings were concerned, it was empty, utterly empty. No one sat in the chairs; no one stood on the mat before the fire; there was no sign even that a patient was anywhere close against the wall, examining the Bocklin reproductions—as patients so often did when they thought they were alone—and therefore rather difficult to see from the spy-hole. Ordinarily speaking, there was no one in the room. It was undeniable.

Yet Dr. Silence was quite well aware that a human being *was* in the room. His psychic apparatus never failed in letting him know the proximity of an incarnate or discarnate being. Even in the dark he could tell that. And he now knew positively that his patient—the patient who had alarmed Barker, and had then tripped down the corridor with that dancing footstep—was somewhere concealed within the four walls commanded by his spy-hole. He also realised—and this was most unusual—that this individual whom he desired to watch knew that he was being watched. And, further, that the stranger himself was also watching! In fact, that it was he, the doctor, who was being observed—and by an observer as keen and trained as himself.

An inkling of the true state of the case began to dawn upon him, and he was on the verge of entering—indeed, his hand already touched the door-knob—when his eye, still glued to the spy-hole, detected a slight movement. Directly opposite, between him and the fireplace, something stirred. He watched very attentively and made certain that he was not mistaken. An object on the mantelpiece—it was a blue vase—disappeared from view. It passed out of sight together with the portion of the marble mantelpiece on which it rested. Next, that part of the fire and grate and brass fender immediately below it vanished entirely, as though a slice had been taken clean out of them.

Dr. Silence then understood that something between him and these objects was slowly coming into being, something that concealed them and obstructed his vision by inserting itself in the line of sight between them and himself.

He quietly awaited further results before going in.

First he saw a thin perpendicular line tracing itself from just above the height of the clock and continuing downwards till it reached the woolly fire-mat. This line grew wider, broadened, grew solid. It was no shadow; it was something substantial. It defined itself more and more. Then suddenly, at the top of the line, and about on a level with the face of the clock, he saw a round luminous disc gazing steadily at him. It was a human eye, looking straight into his own, pressed there against the spy-hole. And it was bright with intelligence. Dr. Silence held his breath for a moment—and stared back at it.

Then, like some one moving out of deep shadow into light, he saw the figure of a man come sliding sideways into view, a whitish face following the eye, and the perpendicular line he had first observed broadening out and developing into the complete figure of a human being. It was the patient. He had apparently been standing there in front of the fire all the time. A second eye had followed the first, and both of them stared steadily at the spy-hole, sharply concentrated, yet with a sly twinkle of humour and amusement that made it impossible for the doctor to maintain his position any longer.

He opened the door and went in quickly. As he did so he noticed for the first time the sound of a German band coming in gaily through the open ventilators. In some intuitive, unaccountable fashion the music connected itself with the patient he was about to interview. This sort of prevision was not unfamiliar to him. It always explained itself later.

The man, he saw, was of middle age and of very ordinary appearance; so ordinary, in fact, that he was difficult to describe—his only peculiarity being his extreme thinness. Pleasant—that is, good—vibrations issued from his atmosphere and met Dr. Silence as he advanced to greet him, yet vibrations alive with currents and discharges betraying the perturbed and disordered condition of his mind and brain. There was evidently something wholly out of the usual in the state of his thoughts. Yet, though strange, it was not altogether distressing; it was not the impression that the broken and violent atmosphere of the insane produces upon the mind. Dr. Silence realised in a flash that here was a case of absorbing interest that might require all his powers to handle properly.

"I was watching you through my little peep-hole—as you saw," he began, with a pleasant smile, advancing to shake hands. "I find it of the greatest assistance sometimes—"

But the patient interrupted him at once. His voice was hurried and had odd, shrill changes in it, breaking from high to low in unexpected fashion. One moment it thundered, the next it almost squeaked.

"I understand without explanation," he broke in rapidly. "You get the true note of a man in this way—when he thinks himself unobserved. I quite agree. Only, in my case, I fear, you saw very little. My case, as you of course grasp, Dr. Silence, is extremely peculiar, uncomfortably peculiar. Indeed, unless Sir William had positively assured me—"

"My friend has sent you to me," the doctor interrupted gravely, with a gentle note of authority, "and that is quite sufficient. Pray, be seated, Mr.—"

"Mudge—Racine Mudge," returned the other.

"Take this comfortable one, Mr. Mudge," leading him to the fixed chair, "and tell me your condition in your own way and at your own pace. My whole day is at your service if you require it."

Mr. Mudge moved towards the chair in question and then hesitated.

"You will promise me not to use the narcotic buttons," he said, before sitting down. "I do not need them. Also I ought to mention that anything you think of vividly will reach my mind. That is apparently part of my peculiar case." He sat down with a sigh and arranged his thin legs and body into a position of comfort. Evidently he was very sensitive to the thoughts of others, for the picture of the green buttons had only entered the doctor's mind for a second, yet the other had instantly snapped it up. Dr. Silence noticed, too, that Mr. Mudge held on tightly with both hands to the arms of the chair.

"I'm rather glad the chair is nailed to the floor," he remarked, as he settled himself more comfortably. "It suits me admirably. The fact is—and this is my case in a nutshell—which is all that a doctor of your marvellous development requires—the fact is, Dr. Silence, I am a victim of Higher Space. That's what's the matter with me— Higher Space!"

The two looked at each other for a space in silence, the little patient holding tightly to the arms of the chair which "suited him admirably," and looking up with staring eyes, his atmosphere positively trembling with the waves of some unknown activity; while the doctor smiled kindly and sympathetically, and put his whole person as far as possible into the mental condition of the other.

"Higher Space," repeated Mr. Mudge, "that's what it is. Now, do you think you can help me with *that*?"

There was a pause during which the men's eyes steadily searched down below the surface of their respective personalities. Then Dr. Silence spoke.

"I am quite sure I can help," he answered quietly; "sympathy must always help, and suffering always owns my sympathy. I see you have suffered cruelly. You must tell me all about your case, and when I hear the gradual steps by which you reached this strange condition, I have no doubt I can be of assistance to you."

He drew a chair up beside his interlocutor and laid a hand on his shoulder for a moment. His whole being radiated kindness, intelligence, desire to help.

"For instance," he went on, "I feel sure it was the result of no mere chance that you became familiar with the terrors of what you term Higher Space; for Higher Space is no mere external measurement. It is, of course, a spiritual state, a spiritual condition, an inner development, and one that we must recognise as abnormal, since it is beyond the reach of the world at the present stage of evolution. Higher Space is a mythical state."

"Oh!" cried the other, rubbing his birdlike hands with pleasure, "the relief it is to be able to talk to some one who can understand! Of course what you say is the utter truth. And you are right that no mere chance led me to my present condition, but, on the other hand, prolonged and deliberate study. Yet chance in a sense now governs it. I mean, my entering the condition of Higher Space seems to depend upon the chance of this and that circumstance. For instance, the mere sound of that German band sent me off. Not that all music will do so, but certain sounds, certain vibrations, at once key me up to the requisite pitch, and off I go. Wagner's music always does it, and that band must have been playing a stray bit of Wagner. But I'll come to all that later. Only first, I must ask you to send away your man from the spy-hole."

John Silence looked up with a start, for Mr. Mudge's back was to the door, and there was no mirror. He saw the brown eye of Barker glued to the little circle of glass, and he crossed the room without a word and snapped down the black shutter provided for the purpose, and then heard Barker snuffle away along the passage.

"Now," continued the little man in the chair, "I can begin. You have managed to put me completely at my ease, and I feel I may tell you my whole case without shame or reserve. You will understand. But you must be patient with me if I go into details that are already familiar to you—details of Higher Space, I mean—and if I seem stupid when I have to describe things that transcend the power of language and are really therefore indescribable."

"My dear friend," put in the other calmly, "that goes without saying. To know Higher Space is an experience that defies description, and one is obliged to make use of more or less intelligible symbols. But, pray, proceed. Your vivid thoughts will tell me more than your halting words."

An immense sigh of relief proceeded from the little figure half lost in the depths of the chair. Such intelligent sympathy meeting him half-way was a new experience to him, and it touched his heart at once. He leaned back, relaxing his tight hold of the arms, and began in his thin, scale-like voice.

"My mother was a Frenchwoman, and my father an Essex bargeman," he said abruptly. "Hence my name—Racine and Mudge. My father died before I ever saw him. My mother inherited money from her Bordeaux relations, and when she died soon after, I was left alone with wealth and a strange freedom. I had no guardian, trustees, sisters, brothers, or any connection in the world to look after me. I grew up, therefore, utterly without education. This much was to my advantage; I learned none of that deceitful rubbish taught in schools, and so had nothing to unlearn when I awakened to my true love—mathematics, higher mathematics and higher geometry. These, however, I seemed to know instinctively. It was like the memory of what I had deeply studied before; the principles were in my blood, and I simply raced through the ordinary stages, and beyond, and then did the same with geometry. Afterwards, when I read the books on these subjects, I understood how swift and undeviating the knowledge had come back to me. It was simply memory. It was simply *re-collecting* the memories of what I had known before in a previous existence and required no books to teach me."

In his growing excitement, Mr. Mudge attempted to drag the chair forward a little nearer to his listener, and then smiled faintly as he resigned himself instantly again to its immovability, and plunged anew into the recital of his singular "disease."

"The audacious speculations of Bolyai, the amazing theories of Gauss—that through a point more than one line could be drawn parallel to a given line; the possibility that the angles of a triangle are together *greater* than two right angles, if drawn upon immense curvatures—the breathless intuitions of Beltrami and Lobatchewsky—all these I hurried through, and emerged, panting but unsatisfied, upon the verge of my—my new world, my Higher Space possibilities—in a word, my disease!

"How I got there," he resumed after a brief pause, during which he appeared to be listening intently for an approaching sound, "is more than I can put intelligibly into words. I can only hope to leave your mind with an intuitive comprehension of the possibility of what I say.

"Here, however, came a change. At this point I was no longer absorbing the fruits of studies I had made before; it was the beginning of new efforts to learn for the first time, and I had to go slowly and laboriously through terrible work. Here I sought for the theories and speculations of others. But books were few and far between, and with the exception of one man—a 'dreamer,' the world called him—whose audacity and piercing intuition amazed and delighted me beyond description, I found no one to guide or help.

"You, of course, Dr. Silence, understand something of what I am driving at with these stammering words, though you cannot perhaps yet guess what depths of pain my new knowledge brought me to, nor why an acquaintance with a new development of space should prove a source of misery and terror."

Mr. Racine Mudge, remembering that the chair would not move, did the next best thing he could in his desire to draw nearer to the attentive man facing him, and sat forward upon the very edge of the cushions, crossing his legs and gesticulating with both hands as though he saw into this region of new space he was attempting to describe, and might any moment tumble into it bodily from the edge of the chair and disappear form view. John Silence, separated from him by three paces, sat with his eyes fixed upon the thin white face opposite, noting every word and every gesture with deep attention.

"This room we now sit in, Dr. Silence, has one side open to space—to Higher Space. A closed box only *seems* closed. There is a way in and out of a soap bubble without breaking the skin."

"You tell me no new thing," the doctor interposed gently.

"Hence, if Higher Space exists and our world borders upon it and lies partially in it, it follows necessarily that we see only portions of all objects. We never see their true and complete shape. We see their three measurements, but not their fourth. The new direction is concealed from us, and when I hold this book and move my hand all round it I have not really made a complete circuit. We only perceive those portions of any object which exist in our three dimensions; the rest escapes us. But, once we learn to see in Higher Space, objects will appear as they actually are. Only they will thus be hardly recognisable!

"Now, you may begin to grasp something of what I am coming to."

"I am beginning to understand something of what you must have suffered," observed the doctor soothingly, "for I have made similar experiments myself, and only stopped just in time—"

"You are the one man in all the world who can hear and understand, *and* sympathise," exclaimed Mr. Mudge, grasping his hand and holding it tightly while he spoke. The nailed chair prevented further excitability.

"Well," he resumed, after a moment's pause, "I procured the implements and the coloured blocks for practical experiment, and I followed the instructions carefully till I had arrived at a working conception of four-dimensional space. The tesseract, the figure whose boundaries are cubes, I knew by heart. That is to say, I knew it and saw it mentally, for my eye, of course, could never take in a new measurement, or my hands and feet handle it.

"So, at least, I thought," he added, making a wry face. "I had reached the stage, you see, when I could imagine in a new dimension. I was able to conceive the shape of that new figure which is intrinsically different to all we know—the shape of the tesseract. I could perceive in four dimensions. When, therefore, I looked at a cube I could see all its sides at once. Its top was not foreshortened, nor its farther side and base invisible. I saw the whole thing out flat, so to speak. And this tesseract was bounded by cubes! Moreover, I also saw its content—its insides."

"You were not yourself able to enter this new world," interrupted Dr. Silence.

"Not then. I was only able to conceive intuitively what it was like and how exactly it must look. Later, when I slipped in there and saw objects in their entirety, unlimited by the paucity of our poor three measurements, I very nearly lost my life. For, you see, space does not stop at a single new dimension, a fourth. It extends in all possible new ones, and we must conceive it as containing any number of new dimensions. In other words, there is no space at all, but only a spiritual condition. But, meanwhile, I had come to grasp the strange fact that the objects in our normal world appear to us only partially."

Mr. Mudge moved farther forward till he was balanced dangerously on the very edge of the chair. "From this starting point," he resumed, "I began my studies and experiments, and continued them for years. I had money, and I was without friends. I lived in solitude and experimented. My intellect, of course, had little part in the work, for intellectually it was all unthinkable. Never was the limitation of mere reason more plainly demonstrated. It was mystically, intuitively, spiritually that I began to advance. And what I learnt, and knew, and did is all impossible to put into language, since it all describes experiences transcending the experiences of men. It is only some of the results—what you would call the symptoms of my disease—that I can give you, and even these must often appear absurd contradictions and impossible paradoxes.

"I can only tell you, Dr. Silence"—his manner became exceedingly impressive—"that I reached sometimes a point of view whence all the great puzzle of the world became plain to me, and I understood what they call in the Yoga books 'The Great Heresy of Separateness'; why all great teachers have urged the necessity of man loving his neighbour as himself; how men are all really one; and why the utter loss of self is necessary to salvation and the discovery of the true life of the soul."

He paused a moment and drew breath.

"Your speculations have been my own long ago," the doctor said quietly. "I fully realise the force of your words. Men are doubtless not separate at all—in the sense they imagine—"

"All this about the very much Higher Space I only dimly, very dimly, conceived, of course," the other went on, raising his voice again by jerks; "but what did happen to me was the humbler accident of—the simpler disaster—oh, dear, how shall I put it—?"

He stammered and showed visible signs of distress.

"It was simply this," he resumed with a sudden rush of words, "that, accidentally, as the result of my years of experiment, I one day slipped bodily into the next world, the world of four dimensions, yet without knowing precisely how I got there, or how I could get back again. I discovered, that is, that my ordinary three-dimensional body was but an expression—a projection—of my higher four-dimensional body!

"Now you understand what I meant much earlier in our talk when I spoke of chance. I cannot control my entrance or exit. Certain people, certain human atmospheres, certain wandering forces, thoughts, desires even—the radiations of certain combinations of colour, and above all, the vibrations of certain kinds of music, will suddenly throw me into a state of what I can only describe as an intense and terrific inner vibration—and behold I am off! Off in the direction at right angles to all our known directions! Off in the direction the cube takes when it begins to trace the outlines of the new figure! Off into my breathless and semi-divine Higher Space! Off, *inside myself*, into the world of four dimensions!"

He gasped and dropped back into the depths of the immovable chair.

"And there," he whispered, his voice issuing from among the cushions, "there I have to stay until these vibrations subside, or until they do something which I cannot find words to describe properly or intelligibly to you—and then, behold, I am back again. First, that is, I disappear. Then I reappear."

"Just so," exclaimed Dr. Silence, "and that is why a few—"

"Why a few moments ago," interrupted Mr. Mudge, taking the words out of his mouth, "you found me gone, and then saw me return. The music of that wretched German band sent me off. Your intense thinking about me brought me back—when the band had stopped its Wagner. I saw you approach the peep-hole and I saw Barker's intention of doing so later. For me no interiors are hidden. I see inside. When in that state the content of your mind, as of your body, is open to me as the day. Oh, dear, oh, dear, oh, dear!"

Mr. Mudge stopped and again mopped his brow. A light trembling ran over the surface of his small body like wind over grass. He still held tightly to the arms of the chair.

"At first," he presently resumed, "my new experiences were so vividly interesting that I felt no alarm. There was no room for it. The alarm came a little later."

"Then you actually penetrated far enough into that state to experience yourself as a normal portion of it?" asked the doctor, leaning forward, deeply interested.

Mr. Mudge nodded a perspiring face in reply.

"I did," he whispered, "undoubtedly I did. I am coming to all that. It began first at night, when I realised that sleep brought no loss of consciousness—"

"The spirit, of course, can never sleep. Only the body becomes unconscious," interposed John Silence.

"Yes, we know that—theoretically. At night, of course, the spirit is active elsewhere, and we have no memory of where and how, simply because the brain stays behind and receives no record. But I found that, while remaining conscious, I also retained memory. I had attained to the state of continuous consciousness, for at night I regularly, with the first approaches of drowsiness, entered *nolens volens* the four-dimensional world.

"For a time this happened regularly, and I could not control it; though later I found a way to regulate it better. Apparently sleep is unnecessary in the higher—the four-dimensional—body. Yes, perhaps. But I should infinitely have preferred dull sleep to the knowledge. For, unable to control my movements, I wandered to and fro, attracted, owing to my partial development and premature arrival, to parts of this new world that alarmed me more and more. It was the awful waste and drift of a monstrous world, so utterly different to all we know and see that I cannot even hint at the nature of the sights and objects and beings in it. More than that, I cannot even remember them. I cannot now picture them to myself even, but can recall only the *memory of the impression* they made upon me, the horror and devastating terror of it all. To be in several places at once, for instance—"

"Perfectly," interrupted John Silence, noticing the increase of the other's excitement, "I understand exactly. But now, please, tell me a little more of this alarm you experienced, and how it affected you."

"It's not the disappearing and reappearing *per se* that I mind," continued Mr. Mudge, "so much as certain other things. It's seeing people and objects in their weird entirety, in their true and complete shapes, that is so distressing. It introduces me to a world of monsters. Horses, dogs, cats, all of which I loved; people, trees, children; all that I have considered beautiful in life—everything, from a human face to a cathedral—appear to me in a different shape and aspect to all I have known before. I cannot perhaps convince you why this should be terrible, but I assure you that it is so. To hear the human voice proceeding from this novel appearance which I scarcely recognise as a human body is ghastly, simply ghastly. To see inside everything and everybody is a form of insight peculiarly distressing. To be so confused in geography as to find myself one moment at the North Pole, and the next at Clapham Junction—or possibly at both places simultaneously—is absurdly terrifying. Your imagination will readily furnish other details without my multiplying my experiences now. But you have no idea what it all means, and how I suffer."

Mr. Mudge paused in his panting account and lay back in his chair. He still held tightly to the arms as though they could keep him in the world of sanity and three measurements, and only now and again released his left hand in order to mop his face. He looked very thin and white and oddly unsubstantial, and he stared about him as though he saw into this other space he had been talking about.

John Silence, too, felt warm. He had listened to every word and had made many notes. The presence of this man had an exhilarating effect upon him. It seemed as if Mr. Racine Mudge still carried about with him something of that breathless Higher-Space condition he had been describing. At any rate, Dr. Silence had himself advanced sufficiently far along the legitimate paths of spiritual and psychic transformations to realise that the visions of this extraordinary little person had a basis of truth for their origin.

After a pause that prolonged itself into minutes, he crossed the room and unlocked a drawer in a bookcase, taking out a small book with a red cover. It had a lock to it, and he produced a key out of his pocket and proceeded to open the covers. The bright eyes of Mr. Mudge never left him for a single second.

"It almost seems a pity," he said at length, "to cure you, Mr. Mudge. You are on the way to discovery of great things. Though you may lose your life in the process— that is, your life here in the world of three dimensions— you would lose thereby nothing of great value—you will pardon my apparent rudeness, I know—and you might gain what is infinitely greater. Your suffering, of course, lies in the fact that you alternate between the two worlds and are never wholly in one or the other. Also, I rather imagine, though I cannot be certain of this from any personal experiments, that you have here and there penetrated even into space of more than four dimensions, and have hence experienced the terror you speak of."

The perspiring son of the Essex bargeman and the woman of Normandy bent his head several times in assent, but uttered no word in reply.

"Some strange psychic predisposition, dating no doubt from one of your former lives, has favoured the development of your 'disease'; and the fact that you had no normal training at school or college, no leading by the poor intellect into the culs-de-sac falsely called knowledge, has further caused your exceedingly rapid movement along the lines of direct inner experience. None of the knowledge you have foreshadowed has come to you through the senses, of course."

Mr. Mudge, sitting in his immovable chair, began to tremble slightly. A wind again seemed to pass over his surface and again to set it curiously in motion like a field of grass.

"You are merely talking to gain time," he said hurriedly, in a shaking voice. "This thinking aloud delays us. I see ahead what you are coming to, only please be quick, for something is going to happen. A band is again coming down the street, and if it plays—if it plays Wagner—I shall be off in a twinkling."

"Precisely. I will be quick. I was leading up to the point of how to effect your cure. The way is this: You must simply learn to *block the entrances*."

"True, true, utterly true!" exclaimed the little man, dodging about nervously in the depths of the chair. "But how, in the name of space, is that to be done?"

"By concentration. They are all within you, these entrances, although outer cases such as colour, music and other things lead you towards them. These external things you cannot hope to destroy, but once the entrances are blocked, they will lead you only to bricked walls and closed channels. You will no longer be able to find the way."

"Quick, quick!" cried the bobbing figure in the chair. "How is this concentration to be effected?"

"This little book," continued Dr. Silence calmly, "will explain to you the way." He tapped the cover. "Let me now read out to you certain simple instructions, composed, as I see you divine, entirely from my own personal experiences in the same direction. Follow these instructions and you will no longer enter the state of Higher Space. The entrances will be blocked effectively."

Mr. Mudge sat bolt upright in his chair to listen, and John Silence cleared his throat and began to read slowly in a very distinct voice.

But before he had uttered a dozen words, something happened. A sound of street music entered the room through the open ventilators, for a band had begun to play in the stable mews at the back of the house—the March from *Tannhäuser*. Odd as it may seem that a German band should twice within the space of an hour enter the same mews and play Wagner, it was nevertheless the fact.

Mr. Racine Mudge heard it. He uttered a sharp, squeaking cry and twisted his arms with nervous energy round the chair. A piteous look that was not far from tears spread over his white face. Grey shadows followed it—the grey of fear. He began to struggle convulsively.

"Hold me fast! Catch me! For God's sake, keep me here! I'm on the rush already. Oh, it's frightful!" he cried in tones of anguish, his voice as thin as a reed.

Dr. Silence made a plunge forward to seize him, but in a flash, before he could cover the space between them, Mr. Racine Mudge, screaming and struggling, seemed to shoot past him into invisibility. He disappeared like an arrow from a bow propelled at infinite speed, and his voice no longer sounded in the external air, but seemed in some curious way to make itself heard somewhere within the depths of the doctor's own being. It was almost like a faint singing cry in his head, like a voice of dream, a voice of vision and unreality.

"Alcohol, alcohol!" it cried, "give me alcohol! It's the quickest way. Alcohol, before I'm out of reach!"

The doctor, accustomed to rapid decisions and even more rapid action, remembered that a brandy flask stood upon the mantelpiece, and in less than a second he had seized it and was holding it out towards the space above the chair recently occupied by the visible Mudge. Then, before his very eyes, and long ere he could unscrew the metal stopper, he saw the contents of the closed glass phial sink and lessen as though some one were drinking violently and greedily of the liquor within.

"Thanks! Enough! It deadens the vibrations!" cried the faint voice in his interior, as he withdrew the flask and set it back upon the mantelpiece. He understood that in Mudge's present condition one side of the flask was open to space and he could drink without removing the stopper. He could hardly have had a more interesting proof of what he had been hearing described at such length.

But the next moment—the very same moment it almost seemed—the German band stopped midway in its tune—and there was Mr. Mudge back in his chair again, gasping and panting!

"Quick!" he shrieked, "stop that band! Send it away! Catch hold of me! Block the entrances! Block the entrances! Give me the red book! Oh, oh, oh-h-h-h!!!"

The music had begun again. It was merely a temporary interruption. The *Tannhäuser March* started again, this time at a tremendous pace that made it sound like a rapid two-step as though the instruments played against time.

But the brief interruption gave Dr. Silence a moment in which to collect his scattering thoughts, and before the band had got through half a bar, he had flung forward upon the chair and held Mr. Racine Mudge, the struggling little victim of Higher Space, in a grip of iron. His arms went all round his diminutive person, taking in a good part of the chair at the same time. He was not a big man, yet he seemed to smother Mudge completely.

Yet, even as he did so, and felt the wriggling form underneath him, it began to melt and slip away like air or water. The wood of the arm-chair somehow disentangled itself from between his own arms and those of Mudge. The phenomenon known as the passage of matter through matter took place. The little man seemed actually to get mixed up in his own being. Dr. Silence could just see his face beneath him. It puckered and grew dark as though from some great internal effort. He heard the thin, reedy voice cry in his ear to "Block the entrances, block the entrances!" and then—but how in the world describe what is indescribable?

John Silence half rose up to watch. Racine Mudge, his face distorted beyond all recognition, was making a marvellous inward movement, as though doubling back upon himself. He turned funnel-wise like water in a whirling vortex, and then appeared to break up somewhat as a reflection breaks up and divides in a distorting convex mirror. He went neither forward nor backwards, neither to the right nor the left, neither up nor down. But he went. He went utterly. He simply flashed away out of sight like a vanishing projectile.

All but one leg! Dr. Silence just had the time and the presence of mind to seize upon the left ankle and boot as it disappeared, and to this he held on for several seconds like grim death. Yet all the time he knew it was a foolish and useless thing to do.

The foot was in his grasp one moment, and the next it seemed—this was the only way he could describe it—inside his own skin and bones, and at the same time outside his hand and all round it. It seemed mixed up in some amazing way with his own flesh and blood. Then it was gone, and he was tightly grasping a draught of heated air.

"Gone! gone! gone!" cried a thick, whispering voice, somewhere deep within his own consciousness. "Lost! lost! lost!" it repeated, growing fainter and fainter till at length it vanished into nothing and the last signs of Mr. Racine Mudge vanished with it.

John Silence locked his red book and replaced it in the cabinet, which he fastened with a click, and when Barker answered the bell he inquired if Mr. Mudge had left a card upon the table. It appeared that he had, and when the servant returned with it, Dr. Silence read the address and made a note of it. It was in North London.

"Mr. Mudge has gone," he said quietly to Barker, noticing his expression of alarm.

"He's not taken his 'at with him, sir."

"Mr. Mudge requires no hat where he is now," continued the doctor, stooping to poke the fire. "But he may return for it—"

"And the humbrella, sir."

"And the umbrella."

"He didn't go out *my* way, sir, if you please," stuttered the amazed servant, his curiosity overcoming his nervousness.

"Mr. Mudge has his own way of coming and going, and prefers it. If he returns by the door at any time, remember to bring him instantly to me, and be kind and gentle with him and ask no questions. Also, remember, Barker, to think pleasantly, sympathetically, affectionately of him while he is away. Mr. Mudge is a very suffering gentleman."

Barker bowed and went out of the room backwards, gasping and feeling round the inside of his collar with three very hot fingers of one hand.

It was two days later when he brought in a telegram to the study. Dr. Silence opened it, and read as follows:

"Bombay. Just slipped out again. All safe. Have blocked entrances. Thousand thanks. Address Cooks, London. —MUDGE."

Dr. Silence looked up and saw Barker staring at him bewilderingly. It occurred to him that somehow he knew the contents of the telegram.

"Make a parcel of Mr. Mudge's things," he said briefly, "and address them to Thomas Cook & Sons, Ludgate Circus. And send them there exactly a month from to-day and marked 'To be called for.'"

"Yes, sir," said Barker, leaving the room with a deep sigh and a hurried glance at the waste-paper basket where his master had dropped the pink paper.

1914

THE PEOPLE OF THE PIT

A. Merritt

North of us a shaft of light shot half way to the zenith. It came from behind the five peaks. The beam drove up through a column of blue haze whose edges were marked as sharply as the rain that streams from the edges of a thunder cloud. It was like the flash of a searchlight through an azure mist. It cast no shadows.

As it struck upward the summits were outlined hard and black and I saw that the whole mountain was shaped like a hand. As the light silhouetted it, the gigantic fingers stretched, the hand seemed to thrust itself forward. It was exactly as though it moved to push something back. The shining beam held steady for a moment; then broke into myriads of little luminous globes that swung to and fro and dropped gently. They seemed to be searching.

The forest had become very still. Every wood noise held its breath. I felt the dogs pressing against my legs. They too were silent; but every muscle in their bodies trembled, their hair was stiff along their backs and their eyes, fixed on the falling lights, were filmed with the terror glaze.

I looked at Anderson. He was staring at the North where once more the beam had pulsed upward.

"It can't be the aurora." I spoke without moving my lips. My mouth was as dry as though Lao T'zai had poured his fear dust down my throat.

"If it is, I never saw one like it," he answered in the same tone. "Besides, who ever heard of an aurora at this time of the year?"

He voiced the thought that was in my own mind.

"It makes me think something is being hunted up there," he said, "an unholy sort of hunt—it's well for us to be out of range."

"The mountain seems to move each time the shaft shoots up," I said. "What's it keeping back, Starr? It makes me think of the frozen hand of cloud that Shan Nadour set before the Gate of Ghouls to keep them in the lairs that Eblis cut for them."

He raised a hand—listening.

From the North and high overhead there came a whispering. It was not the rustling of the aurora, that rushing, crackling sound like the ghosts of winds that blew at Creation racing through the skeleton leaves of ancient trees that sheltered Lilith. It was a whispering that held in it a demand. It was eager. It called us to come up where the beam was flashing. It drew. There was in it a note of inexorable insistence. It touched my heart with a thousand tiny fear-tipped fingers and it filled me with a vast longing to race on and merge myself in the light. It must have been so that Ulysses felt when he strained at the mast and strove to obey the crystal sweet singing of the Sirens.

The whispering grew louder.

"What the hell's the matter with those dogs?" cried Anderson savagely. "Look at them!"

The malemutes, whining, were racing away toward the light. We saw them disappear among the trees. There came back to us a mournful howling. Then that too died away and left nothing but the insistent murmuring overhead.

The glade we had camped in looked straight to the North. We had reached I suppose three hundred miles above the first great bend of the Koskokwim toward the Yukon. Certainly we were in an untrodden part of the wilderness. We had pushed through from Dawson at the breaking of the Spring, on a fair lead to the lost five peaks between which, so the Athabasean medicine man had told us, the gold streams out like putty from a clenched fist. Not an Indian were we able to get to go with us. The land of the Hand Mountain was accursed, they said. We had sighted the peaks the night before, their tops faintly outlined against a pulsing glow. And now we saw the light that had led us to them.

Anderson stiffened. Through the whispering had broken a curious pad-pad and a rustling. It sounded as though a small bear were moving towards us. I threw a pile of wood on the fire and, as it blazed up, saw something break through the bushes. It walked on all fours, but it did not walk like a bear. All at once it flashed upon me—it was like a baby crawling upstairs. The forepaws lifted themselves in grotesquely infantile fashion. It was grotesque but it was—terrible. It grew closer. We reached for our guns—and dropped them. Suddenly we knew that this crawling thing was a man!

It was a man. Still with the high climbing pad-pad he swayed to the fire. He stopped.

"Safe," whispered the crawling man, in a voice that was an echo of the murmur overhead. "Quite safe here. They can't get out of the blue, you know. They can't get you—unless you go to them—"

He fell over on his side. We ran to him. Anderson knelt.

"God's love!" he said. "Frank, look at this!" He pointed to the hands. The wrists were covered with torn rags of a heavy shirt. The hands themselves were stumps! The fingers had been bent into the palms and the flesh had been worn to the bone. They looked like the feet of a little black elephant! My eyes traveled down the body. Around the waist was a heavy band of yellow metal. From it fell a ring and a dozen links of shining white chain!

"What is he? Where did he come from?" said Anderson. "Look, he's fast asleep—yet even in his sleep his arms try to climb and his feet draw themselves up one after the other! And his knees—how in God's name was he ever able to move on them?"

It was even as he said. In the deep sleep that had come upon the crawler, arms and legs kept raising in a deliberate, dreadful climbing motion. It was as though they had a life of their own—they kept their movement independently of the motionless body. They were semaphoric motions. If you have ever stood at the back of a train and watched the semaphores rise and fall you will know exactly what I mean.

Abruptly the overhead whispering ceased. The shaft of light dropped and did not rise again. The crawling man became still. A gentle glow began to grow around us. It was dawn, and the short Alaskan summer night was over. Anderson rubbed his eyes and turned to me a haggard face.

"Man!" he exclaimed. "You look as though you have been through a spell of sickness!"

"No more than you, Starr," I said. "What do you make of it all?"

"I'm thinking our only answer lies there," he answered, pointing to the figure that lay so motionless under the blankets we had thrown over him. "Whatever it was— that's what it was after. There was no aurora about that light, Frank. It was like the flaring up of some queer hell the preacher folk never frightened us with."

"We'll go no further today," I said. "I wouldn't wake him for all the gold that runs between the fingers of the five peaks—nor for all the devils that may be behind them."

The crawling man lay in a sleep as deep as the Styx. We bathed and bandaged the pads that had been his hands. Arms and legs were as rigid as though they were crutches. He did not move while we worked over him. He lay as he had fallen, the arms a trifle raised, the knees bent.

"Why did he crawl?" whispered Anderson. "Why didn't he walk?"

I was filing the band about the waist. It was gold, but it was like no gold I had ever handled. Pure gold is soft. This was soft, but it had an unclean, viscid life of its own. It clung to the file. I gashed through it, bent it away from the body and hurled it far off. It was—loathsome!

All that day he slept. Darkness came and still he slept. That night there was no shaft of light, no questing globe, no whispering. Some spell of horror seemed lifted from the land. It was noon when the crawling man awoke. I jumped as the pleasant drawling voice sounded.

"How long have I slept?" he asked. His pale blue eyes grew quizzical as I stared at him. "A night—and almost two days," I said. "Was there any light up there last night?" He nodded to the North eagerly. "Any whispering?"

"Neither," I answered. His head fell back and he stared up at the sky.

"They've given it up, then?" he said at last.

"Who have given it up?" asked Anderson.

"Why, the people of the pit," replied the crawling man quietly.

We stared at him. "The people of the pit," he said. "Things that the Devil made before the Flood and that somehow have escaped God's vengeance. You weren't in any danger from them—unless you had followed their call. They can't get any further than the blue haze. I was their prisoner," he added simply. "They were trying to whisper me back to them!"

Anderson and I looked at each other, the same thought in both our minds.

"You're wrong," said the crawling man. "I'm not insane. Give me a very little to drink. I'm going to die soon, but I want you to take me as far South as you can before I die, and afterwards I want you to build a big fire and burn me. I want to be in such shape that no infernal spell of theirs can drag my body back to them. You'll do it too, when I've told you about them . . ." he hesitated. "I think their chain is off me?" he said.

"I cut it off," I answered shortly.

"Thank God for that too," whispered the crawling man.

He drank the brandy and water we lifted to his lips.

"Arms and legs quite dead," he said. "Dead as I'll be soon. Well, they did well for me. Now I'll tell you what's up there behind that hand. Hell!"

"Now listen. My name is Stanton—Sinclair Stanton. Class of 1900, Yale. Explorer. I started away from Dawson last year to hunt for five peaks that rise like a hand in a haunted country and run pure gold between them. Same thing you were after? I thought so. Late last fall my comrade sickened. Sent him back with some Indians. Little later all my Indians ran away from me. I decided I'd stick, built a cabin, stocked myself with food and lay down to winter it. In the Spring I started off again. Little less than two weeks ago I sighted the five peaks. Not from this side though—the other. Give me some more brandy.

"I'd made too wide a detour," he went on. "I'd gotten too far North. I beat back. From this side you see nothing but forest straight up to the base of the Hand Mountain. Over on the other side—"

He was silent for a moment.

"Over there is forest too. But it doesn't reach so far. No! I came out of it. Stretching miles in front of me was a level plain. It was as worn and ancient looking as the desert around the ruins of Babylon. At its end rose the peaks. Between me and them—far off—was what looked like a low dike of rocks. Then—I ran across the road!

"The road!" cried Anderson incredulously.

"The road," said the crawling man. "A fine smooth stone road. It ran straight on to the mountain. Oh, it was road all right—and worn as though millions and millions of feet had passed over it for thousands of years. On each side of it were sand and heaps of stones. After a while I began to notice these stones. They were cut, and the shape of the heaps somehow gave me the idea that a hundred thousand years ago they might have been houses. I sensed man about them and at the same time they smelled of immemorial antiquity. Well—

"The peaks grew closer. The heaps of ruins thicker. Something inexpressibly desolate hovered over them; something reached from them that struck my heart like the touch of ghosts so old that they could be only the ghosts of ghosts. I went on.

"And now I saw that what I had thought to be the low rock range at the base of the peaks was a thicker litter of ruins. The Hand Mountain was really much farther off. The road passed between two high rocks that raised themselves like a gateway."

The crawling man paused.

"They were a gateway," he said. "I reached them. I went between them. And then I sprawled and clutched the earth in sheer awe! I was on a broad stone platform. Before me was—sheer space! Imagine the Grand Canyon five times as wide and with the bottom dropped out. That is what I was looking into. It was like peeping over the edge of a cleft world down into the infinity where the planets roll! On the far side stood the five peaks. They looked like a gigantic warning hand stretched up to the sky. The lip of the abyss curved away on each side of me.

"I could see down perhaps a thousand feet. Then a thick blue haze shut out the eye. It was like the blue you see gather on the high hills at dusk. And the pit—it was awesome; awesome as the Maori Gulf of Ranalak, that sinks between the living and the dead and that only the freshly released soul has strength to leap—but never strength to cross again.

"I crept back from the verge and stood up, weak. My hand rested against one of the pillars of the gateway. There was carving upon it. It bore in still sharp outlines the heroic figure of a man. His back was turned. His arms were outstretched. There was an odd peaked headdress upon him. I looked at the opposite pillar. It bore a figure exactly similar. The pillars were triangular and the carvings were on the side away from the pit. The figures seemed to be holding something back. I looked closer. Behind the outstretched hands I seemed to see other shapes.

"I traced them out vaguely. Suddenly I felt unaccountably sick. There had come to me an impression of enormous upright slugs. Their swollen bodies were faintly cut—all except the heads which were well marked globes. They were—unutterably loathsome. I turned from the gates back to the void. I stretched myself upon the slab and looked over the edge.

"A stairway led down into the pit!"

"A stairway!" we cried.

"A stairway," repeated the crawling man as patiently as before. "It seemed not so much carved out of the rock as built into it. The slabs were about six feet long and three feet wide. It ran down from the platform and vanished into the blue haze."

"But who could build such a stairway as that?" I said. "A stairway built into the wall of a precipice and leading down into a bottomless pit!"

"Not bottomless," said the crawling man quietly. "There was a bottom. I reached it!"

"Reached it?" we repeated.

"Yes, by the stairway," answered the crawling man. "You see—I went down it!

"Yes," he said. "I went down the stairway. But not that day. I made my camp back of the gates. At dawn I filled my knapsack with food, my two canteens with water from a spring that wells up there by the gateway, walked between the carved monoliths and stepped over the edge of the pit.

"The steps ran along the side of the rock at a forty-degree pitch. As I went down and down I studied them. They were of a greenish rock quite different from the granitic porphyry that formed the wall of the precipice. At first I thought that the builders had taken advantage of an outcropping stratum, and had carved from it their gigantic flight. But the regularity of the angle at which it fell made me doubtful of this theory.

"After I had gone perhaps half a mile I stepped out upon a landing. From this landing the stairs made a V shaped turn and ran on downward, clinging to the cliff at the same angle as the first flight; it was a zig-zag, and after I had made three of these turns I knew that the steps dropped straight down in a succession of such angles. No strata could be so regular as that. No, the stairway was built by hands! But whose? The answer is in those ruins around the edge, I think—never to be read.

"By noon I had lost sight of the five peaks and the lip of the abyss. Above me, below me, was nothing but the blue haze. Beside me, too, was nothingness, for the further breast of rock had long since vanished. I felt no dizziness, and any trace of fear was swallowed in a vast curiosity. What was I to discover? Some ancient and wonderful civilization that had ruled when the Poles were tropical gardens? Nothing living, I felt sure—all was too old for life. Still, a stairway so wonderful must lead to something quite as wonderful, I knew. What was it? I went on.

"At regular intervals I had passed the mouths of small caves. There would be two thousand steps and then an opening, two thousand more steps and an opening—and so on and on. Late that afternoon I stopped before one of these clefts. I suppose I had gone then three miles down the pit, although the angles were such that I had walked, in all, fully ten miles. I examined the entrance. On each side were carved the figures of the great portal above, only now they were standing face forward, the arms outstretched as though to hold something back from the outer depths. Their faces were covered with veils. There were no hideous shapes behind them. I went inside. The fissure ran back for twenty yards like a burrow. It was dry and perfectly light. Outside I could see the blue haze rising upward like a column, its edges clearly marked. I felt an extraordinary sense of security, although I had not been conscious of any fear. I felt that the figures at the entrance were guardians—but against what?

"The blue haze thickened and grew faintly luminescent. I fancied that it was dusk above. I ate and drank a little and slept. When I awoke the blue had lightened again, and I fancied it was dawn above. I went on. I forgot the gulf yawning at my side. I felt no fatigue and little hunger or thirst, although I had drunk and eaten sparingly. That night I spent within another of the caves, and at dawn I descended again.

"It was late that day when I first saw the city—."

He was silent for a time.

"The city," he said at last, "there is a city, you know. But not such a city as you have ever seen—nor any other man who has lived to tell of it. The pit, I think, is shaped like a bottle; the opening before the five peaks is the neck. But how wide the bottom is I do not know—thousands of miles maybe. I had begun to catch little glints of light far down in the blue. Then I saw the tops of—trees, I suppose they are. But not our kind of trees—unpleasant, snaky kind of trees. They reared themselves on high thin trunks and their tops were nests of thick tendrils with ugly little leaves like arrow heads. The trees were red, a vivid angry red. Here and there I glimpsed spots of shining yellow. I knew these were water because I could see things breaking through their surface—or at least I could see the splash and ripple, but what it was that disturbed them I never saw.

"Straight beneath me was the—city. I looked down upon mile after mile of closely packed cylinders. They lay upon their sides in pyramids of three, of five—of dozens—piled upon each other. It is hard to make you see what that city is like—look, suppose you have water pipes of a certain length and first you lay three of them side by side and

A. Merritt

on top of them you place two and on these two one; or suppose you take five for a foundation and place on these four and then three, then two and then one. Do you see? That was the way they looked. But they were topped by towers, by minarets, by flares, by fans, and twisted monstrosities. They gleamed as though coated with pale rose flame. Beside them the venomous red trees raised themselves like the heads of hydras guarding nests of gigantic, jeweled and sleeping worms!

"A few feet beneath me the stairway jutted out into a Titanic arch, unearthly as the span that bridges Hell and leads to Asgard. It curved out and down straight through the top of the highest pile of carven cylinders and then it vanished through it. It was appalling—it was demonic—"

The crawling man stopped. His eyes rolled up into his head. He trembled and his arms and legs began their horrible crawling movement. From his lips came a whispering. It was an echo of the high murmuring we had heard the night he came to us. I put my hands over his eyes. He quieted.

"The Things Accursed!" he said. "The People of the Pit! Did I whisper? Yes—but they can't get me now—they can't!"

After a time he began as quietly as before.

"I crossed the span. I went down through the top of that—building. Blue darkness shrouded me for a moment and I felt the steps twist into a spiral. I wound down and then—I was standing high up in—I can't tell you in what, I'll have to call it a room. We have no images for what is in the pit. A hundred feet below me was the floor. The walls sloped down and out from where I stood in a series of widening crescents. The place was colossal—and it was filled with a curious mottled red light. It was like the light inside a green and gold flecked fire opal. I went down to the last step. Far in front of me rose a high, columned altar. Its pillars were carved in monstrous scrolls—like mad octopuses with a thousand drunken tentacles; they rested on the backs of shapeless monstrosities carved in crimson stone. The altar front was a gigantic slab of purple covered with carvings.

"I can't describe these carvings! No human being could—the human eye cannot grasp them any more than it can grasp the shapes that haunt the fourth dimension. Only a subtle sense in the back of the brain sensed them vaguely. They were formless things that gave no conscious image, yet pressed into the mind like small hot seals— ideas of hate—of combats between unthinkable monstrous things—victories in a nebulous hell of steaming, obscene jungles—aspirations and ideals immeasurably loathsome—

"And as I stood I grew aware of something that lay behind the lip of the altar fifty feet above me. I knew it was there—I felt it with every hair and every tiny bit of my skin. Something infinitely malignant, infinitely horrible, infinitely ancient. It lurked, it brooded, it threatened and it—was invisible!

"Behind me was a circle of blue light. I ran for it. Something urged me to turn back, to climb the stairs and make away. It was impossible. Repulsion for that unseen Thing raced me onward as though a current had my feet. I passed through the circle. I was out on a street that stretched on into dim distance between rows of the carven cylinders.

"Here and there the red trees arose. Between them rolled the stone burrows. And now I could take in the amazing ornamentation that clothed them. They were like the trunks of smooth skinned trees that had fallen and had been clothed with high reaching noxious orchids. Yes—those cylinders were like that—and more. They should have gone out with the dinosaurs. They were—monstrous. They struck the eyes like a blow and they passed across the nerves like a rasp. And nowhere was there sight or sound of living thing.

"There were circular openings in the cylinders like the circle in the Temple of the Stairway. I passed through one of them. I was in a long, bare vaulted room whose curving sides half closed twenty feet over my head, leaving a wide slit that opened into another vaulted chamber above. There was absolutely nothing in the room save the same mottled reddish light that I had seen in the Temple. I stumbled. I still could see nothing, but there was something on the floor over which I had tripped. I reached down—and my hand touched a thing cold and smooth—that moved under it—I turned and ran out of that place—I was filled with a loathing that had in it something of madness—I ran on and on blindly—wringing my hands—weeping with horror—

"When I came to myself I was still among the stone cylinders and red trees. I tried to retrace my steps; to find the Temple. I was more than afraid. I was like a new-loosed soul panic-stricken with the first terrors of hell. I could not find the Temple! Then the haze began to thicken and glow; the cylinders to shine more brightly. I knew that it was dusk in the world above and I felt that with dusk my time of peril had come; that the thickening of the haze was the signal for the awakening of whatever things lived in this pit.

"I scrambled up the sides of one of the burrows. I hid behind a twisted nightmare of stone. Perhaps, I thought, there was a chance of remaining hidden until the blue lightened and the peril passed. There began to grow around me a murmur. It was everywhere—and it grew and grew into a great whispering. I peeped from the side of the stone down into the street. I saw lights passing and repassing. More and more lights—they swam out of the circular doorways and they thronged the street. The highest were eight feet above the pavement; the lowest perhaps two. They hurried, they sauntered, they bowed, they stopped and whispered—and there was nothing under them!"

"Nothing under them!" breathed Anderson.

"No," he went on, "that was the terrible part of it—there was nothing under them. Yet certainly the lights were living things. They had consciousness, volition, thought—what else I did not know. They were nearly two feet across—the largest. Their center was a bright nucleus—red, blue, green. This nucleus faded off, gradually, into a misty glow that did not end abruptly. It too seemed to fade off into nothingness—but a nothingness that had under it a somethingness. I strained my eyes trying to grasp this body into which the lights merged and which one could only *feel* was there, but could not *see*.

"And all at once I grew rigid. Something cold, and thin like a whip, had touched my face. I turned my head. Close behind were three of the lights. They were a pale blue. They looked at me—if you can imagine lights that are eyes. Another whiplash gripped my shoulder. Under the closest light came a shrill whispering. I shrieked. Abruptly the murmuring in the street ceased. I dragged my eyes from the pale blue globe that held them and looked out—the lights in the streets were rising by myriads to the level of where I stood! There they stopped and peered at me. They crowded and jostled as though they were a crowd of curious people—on Broadway. I felt a score of the lashes touch me—

"When I came to myself I was again in the great Place of the Stairway, lying at the foot of the altar. All was silent. There were no lights—only the mottled red glow. I jumped to my feet and ran toward the steps. Something jerked me back to my knees. And then I saw that around my waist had been fastened a yellow ring of metal. From it hung a chain and this chain passed up over the lip of the high ledge. I was chained to the altar!

"I reached into my pockets for my knife to cut through the ring. It was not there! I had been stripped of everything except one of the canteens that I had hung around my neck and which I suppose they had thought was—part of me. I tried to break the ring. It seemed alive. It writhed in my hands and it drew itself closer around me! I pulled at the chain. It was immovable. There came to me the consciousness of the unseen Thing above the altar. I groveled at the foot of the slab and wept. Think—alone in that place of strange light with the brooding ancient Horror above me—a monstrous Thing, a Thing unthinkable—an unseen Thing that poured forth horror—

"After a while I gripped myself. Then I saw beside one of the pillars a yellow bowl filled with a thick white liquid. I drank it. If it killed me I did not care. But its taste was pleasant and as I drank my strength came back to me with a rush. Clearly I was not to be starved. The lights, whatever they were, had a conception of human needs.

"And now the reddish mottled gleam began to deepen. Outside arose the humming and through the circle that was the entrance came streaming the globes. They ranged themselves in ranks until they filled the Temple. Their whispering grew into a chant, a cadenced whispering chant that rose and fell, rose and fell, while to its rhythm the globes lifted and sank, lifted and sank.

"All that night the lights came and went—and all that night the chant sounded as they rose and fell. At the last I felt myself only an atom of consciousness in a sea of cadenced whispering; an atom that rose and fell with the bowing globes. I tell you that even my heart pulsed in unison with them! The red glow faded, the lights streamed out; the whispering died. I was again alone and I knew that once again day had broken in my own world.

"I slept. When I awoke I found beside the pillar more of the white liquid. I scrutinized the chain that held me to the altar. I began to rub two of the links together. I did this for hours. When the red began to thicken there was a ridge worn in the links. Hope rushed up within me. There was, then, a chance to escape.

"With the thickening, the lights came again. All through that night the whispering chant sounded, and the globes rose and fell. The chant seized me. It pulsed through me until every nerve and muscle quivered to it. My lips began to quiver. They strove like a man trying to cry out in a nightmare. And at last they too were whispering the chant of the people of the pit. My body bowed in unison with the lights—I was, in movement and sound, one with the nameless things while my soul sank back sick with horror and powerlessness. While I whispered I—saw Them!"

"Saw the lights?" I asked stupidly.

"Saw the Things under the lights," he answered. "Great transparent snail-like bodies—dozens of waving tentacles stretching from them—round gaping mouths under the luminous seeing globes. They were like the ghosts of inconceivably monstrous slugs! I could see through them. And as I stared, still bowing and whispering, the dawn came and they streamed to and through the entrance. They did not crawl or walk—they floated! They floated and were—gone!

"I did not sleep. I worked all that day at my chain. By the thickening of the red I had worn it a sixth through. And all that night I whispered and bowed with the pit people, joining in their chant to the Thing that brooded above me!

"Twice again the red thickened and the chant held me— then on the morning of the fifth day I broke through the worn links of the chain. I was free! I drank from the bowl of white liquid and poured what was left in my flask. I ran to the Stairway. I rushed up and past that unseen Horror behind the altar ledge and was out upon the Bridge. I raced across the span and up the Stairway.

"Can you think what it is to climb straight up the verge of a cleft-world—with hell behind you? Hell was behind me and terror rode me. The city had long been lost in the blue haze before I knew that I could climb no more. My heart beat upon my ears like a sledge. I fell before one of the little caves, feeling that here at last was sanctuary. I crept far back within it and waited for the haze to thicken. Almost at once it did so. From far below me came a vast and angry murmur. At the mouth of the rift I saw a light pulse up through the blue; die down and as it dimmed I saw myriads of the globes that are the eyes of the pit people swing downward into the abyss. Again and again the light pulsed and the globes fell. They were hunting me. The whispering grew louder, more insistent.

"There grew in me the dreadful desire to join in the whispering as I had done in the Temple. I bit my lips through and through to still them. All that night the beam shot up through the abyss, the globes swung and the whispering sounded—and now I knew the purpose of the caves and of the sculptured figures that still had power to guard them. But what were the people who had carved them? Why had they built their city around the verge and why had they set that Stairway in the pit? What had they been to those Things that dwelt at the bottom and what use had the Things been to them that they should live beside their dwelling place? That there had been some purpose was certain. No work so prodigious as the Stairway would have been undertaken otherwise. But what was the purpose? And why was it that those who had dwelt about the abyss had passed away ages gone, and the dwellers in the abyss still lived? I could find no answer—nor can I find any now. I have not the shred of a theory.

"Dawn came as I wondered and with it silence. I drank what was left of the liquid in my canteen, crept from the cave and began to climb again. That afternoon my legs gave out. I tore off my shirt, made from it pads for my knees and coverings for my hands. I crawled upward. I crawled up and up. And again I crept into one of the caves and waited until again the blue thickened, the shaft of light shot through it and the whispering came.

"But now there was a new note in the whispering. It was no longer threatening. It called and coaxed. It drew.

"A new terror gripped me. There had come upon me a mighty desire to leave the cave and go out where the lights swung; to let them do with me as they pleased, carry me where they wished. The desire grew. It gained fresh impulse with every rise of the beam until at last I vibrated with the desire as I had vibrated to the chant in the Temple. My body was a pendulum. Up would go the beam and I would swing toward it! Only my soul kept steady. It held me fast to the floor of the cave; And all that night it fought with my body against the spell of the pit people.

"Dawn came. Again I crept from the cave and faced the Stairway. I could not rise. My hands were torn and bleeding; my knees an agony. I forced myself upward step by step. After a while my hands became numb, the pain left my knees. They deadened. Step by step my will drove my body upward upon them."

"And then—a nightmare of crawling up infinite stretches of steps—memories of dull horror while hidden within caves with the lights pulsing without and whisperings that called and called me—memory of a time when I awoke to find that my body was obeying the call and had carried me half way out between the guardians of the portals while thousands of gleaming globes rested in the blue haze and watched me.

"Glimpses of bitter fights against sleep and always, always—a climb up and up along infinite distances of steps that led from Abaddon to a Paradise of blue sky and open world!

"At last a consciousness of the clear sky close above me, the lip of the pit before me—memory of passing between the great portals of the pit and of steady withdrawal from it—dreams of giant men with strange peaked crowns and veiled faces who pushed me onward and onward and held back Roman Candle globules of light that sought to draw me back to a gulf wherein planets swam between the branches of red trees that had snakes for crowns."

"And then a long, long sleep—how long God alone knows—in a cleft of rocks; an awakening to see far in the North the beam still rising and falling, the lights still hunting, the whispering high above me calling.

"Again crawling on dead arms and legs that moved—that moved—like the Ancient Mariner's ship—without volition of mine, but that carried me from a haunted place. And then—your fire—and this—safety!"

The crawling man smiled at us for a moment. Then swiftly life faded from his face. He slept.

A. Merritt

That afternoon we struck camp and carrying the crawling man started back South. For three days we carried him and still he slept. And on the third day, still sleeping, he died. We built a great pile of wood and we burned his body as he had asked. We scattered his ashes about the forest with the ashes of the trees that had consumed him. It must be a great magic indeed that could disentangle those ashes and draw him back in a rushing cloud to the pit he called Accursed. I do not think that even the People of the Pit have such a spell. No.

But we did not return to the five peaks to see. And if the gold does stream out between the five peaks of the Hand Mountain, like putty from a clenched fist—there it may remain for all of us.

1918

THE THING FROM—'OUTSIDE'

George Allan England

They sat about their camp-fire, that little party of Americans retreating southward from Hudson Bay before the oncoming menace of the great cold. Sat there, stolid under the awe of the North, under the uneasiness that the day's trek had laid upon their souls. The three men smoked. The two women huddled close to each other. Fireglow picked their faces from the gloom of night among the dwarf firs. A splashing murmur told of the Albany River's haste to escape from the wilderness, and reach the Bay.

"I don't see what there was in a mere circular print on a rock-ledge to make our guides desert," said Professor Thorburn. His voice was as dry as his whole personality. "Most extraordinary."

"*They* knew what it was, all right," answered Jandron, geologist of the party. "So do I." He rubbed his cropped mustache. His eyes glinted grayly. "I've seen prints like that before. That was on the Labrador. And I've seen things happen, where they were."

"Something surely happened to our guides, before they'd got a mile into the bush," put in the Professor's wife; while Vivian, her sister, gazed into the fire that revealed her as a beauty, not to be spoiled even by a tam and a rough-knit sweater. "Men don't shoot wildly, and scream like that, unless—"

"They're all three dead now, anyhow," put in Jandron. "So they're out of harm's way. While we—well, we're two hundred and fifty wicked miles from the C.P.R. rails."

"Forget it, Jandy!" said Marr, the journalist. "We're just suffering from an attack of nerves, that's all. Give me a fill of 'baccy. Thanks. We'll all be better in the morning. Ho-hum! Now, speaking of spooks and such—"

He launched into an account of how he had once exposed a fraudulent spiritualist, thus proving—to his own satisfaction—that nothing existed beyond the scope of mankind's everyday life. But nobody gave him much heed. And silence fell upon the little night-encampment in the wilds; a silence that was ominous.

Pale, cold stars watched down from spaces infinitely far beyond man's trivial world.

Next day, stopping for chow on a ledge miles upstream, Jandron discovered another of the prints. He cautiously summoned the other two men. They examined the print, while the women-folk were busy by the fire. A harmless thing the marking seemed; only a ring about four inches in diameter, a kind of cup-shaped depression with a raised center. A sort of glaze coated it, as if the granite had been fused by heat.

Jandron knelt, a well-knit figure in bright mackinaw and canvas leggings, and with a shaking finger explored the smooth curve of the print in the rock. His brows contracted as he studied it.

"We'd better get along out of this as quick as we can," said he in an unnatural voice. "You've got your wife to protect, Thorburn, and I,—well, I've got Vivian. And—"

"You have?" nipped Marr. The light of an evil jealousy gleamed in his heavy-lidded look. "What you need is an alienist."

"Really, Jandron," the Professor admonished, "you mustn't let your imagination run away with you."

"I suppose it's imagination that keeps this print cold!" the geologist retorted. His breath made faint, swirling coils of vapor above it.

"Nothing but a pot-hole," judged Thorburn, bending his spare, angular body to examine the print. The Professor's vitality all seemed centered in his big-bulged skull that sheltered a marvellous thinking machine. Now he put his lean hand to the base of his brain, rubbing the back of his head as if it ached. Then, under what seemed some powerful compulsion, he ran his bony finger around the print in the rock.

"By Jove, but it is cold!" he admitted. "And looks as if it had been stamped right out of the stone. Extraordinary!"

"Dissolved out, you mean," corrected the geologist. "By cold."

The journalist laughed mockingly.

"Wait till I write this up!" he sneered. "'Noted Geologist Declares Frigid Ghost Dissolves Granite!'"

Jandron ignored him. He fetched a little water from the river and poured it into the print.

"Ice!" ejaculated the Professor. "Solid ice!"

"Frozen in a second," added Jandron, while Marr frankly stared.

"And it'll never melt, either. I tell you, I've seen some of these rings before; and every time, horrible things have happened. Incredible things! Something burned this ring out of the stone—burned it out with the cold of interstellar space. Something that can import cold as a permanent quality of matter. Something that can kill matter, and totally remove it."

"Of course that's all sheer poppycock," the journalist tried to laugh, but his brain felt numb.

"This something, this Thing," continued Jandron, "is a Thing that can't be killed by bullets. It's what caught our guides on the barrens, as they ran away—poor fools!"

A shadow fell across the print in the rock. Mrs. Thorburn had come up, was standing there. She had overheard a little of what Jandron had been saying.

"Nonsense!" she tried to exclaim, but she was shivering so she could hardly speak.

That night, after a long afternoon of paddling and portaging—laboring against inhibitions like those in a nightmare—they camped on shelving rocks that slanted to the river.

"After all," said the Professor, when supper was done, "we mustn't get into a panic. I know extraordinary things are reported from the wilderness, and more than one man has come out, raving. But we, by Jove! with our superior brains—we aren't going to let Nature play us any tricks!"

"And of course," added his wife, her arm about Vivian, "everything in the universe is a natural force. There's really no super-natural, at all."

"Admitted," Jandron replied. "But how about things outside the universe?"

"And they call you a scientist?" gibed Marr; but the Professor leaned forward, his brows knit.

"Hm!" he grunted. A little silence fell.

"You don't mean, really," asked Vivian, "that you think there's life and intelligence—Outside?"

Jandron looked at the girl. Her beauty, haloed with ruddy gold from the firelight, was a pain to him as he answered:

"Yes, I do. And dangerous life, too. I know what I've seen, in the North Country. I know what I've seen!"

Silence again, save for the crepitation of the flames, the fall of an ember, the murmur of the current. Darkness narrowed the wilderness to just that circle of flickering light ringed by the forest and the river, brooded over by the pale stars.

"Of course you can't expect a scientific man to take you seriously," commented the Professor.

"I know what I've seen! I tell you there's Something entirely outside man's knowledge."

"Poor fellow!" scoffed the journalist; but even as he spoke his hand pressed his forehead.

"There are Things at work," Jandron affirmed, with dogged persistence. He lighted his pipe with a blazing twig. Its flame revealed his face drawn, lined. "Things. Things that reckon with us no more than we do with ants. Less, perhaps."

The flame of the twig died. Night stood closer, watching.

"Suppose there are?" the girl asked. "What's that got to do with these prints in the rock?"

"*They*," answered Jandron, "are marks left by one of those Things. Footprints, maybe. That Thing is near us, here and now!"

Marr's laugh broke a long stillness.

"And you," he exclaimed, "with an A. M. and a B. S. to write after your name."

"If you knew more," retorted Jandron, "you'd know a devilish sight less. It's only ignorance that's cock-sure."

"But," dogmatized the Professor, "no scientist of any standing has ever admitted any outside interference with this planet."

"No, and for thousands of years nobody ever admitted that the world was round, either. What I've seen, I know."

"Well, what *have* you seen?" asked Mrs. Thorburn, shivering.

"You'll excuse me, please, for not going into that just now."

"You mean," the Professor demanded, dryly, "if the—hm!—this suppositious Thing wants to—?"

"It'll do any infernal thing it takes a fancy to, yes! If it happens to want us—"

"But what *could* Things like that want of us? Why should They come here, at all?"

"Oh, for various reasons. For inanimate objects, at times, and then again for living beings. They've come here lots of times, I tell you," Jandron asserted with strange irritation, "and got what They wanted, and then gone away to—Somewhere. If one of Them happens to want us, for any reason, It will take us, that's all. If It doesn't want us, It will ignore us, as we'd ignore gorillas in Africa if we were looking for gold. But if it was gorilla-fur we wanted, that would be different for the gorillas, wouldn't it?"

"What in the world," asked Vivian, "could a—well, a Thing from Outside want of us?"

"What do men want, say, of guinea-pigs? Men experiment with 'em, of course. Superior beings use inferior, for their own ends. To assume that man is the supreme product of evolution is gross self-conceit. Might not some superior Thing want to experiment with human beings?"

"But how?" demanded Marr.

"The human brain is the most highly-organized form of matter known to this planet. Suppose, now—"

"Nonsense!" interrupted the Professor. "All hands to the sleeping-bags, and no more of this. I've got a wretched headache. Let's anchor in Blanket Bay!"

He, and both the women, turned in. Jandron and Marr sat a while longer by the fire. They kept plenty of wood piled on it, too, for an unnatural chill transfixed the night-air. The fire burned strangely blue, with greenish flicks of flame.

At length, after vast acerbities of disagreement, the geologist and the newspaperman sought their sleeping-bags. The fire was a comfort. Not that a fire could avail a pin's weight against a Thing from interstellar space, but subjectively it was a comfort. The instincts of a million years, centering around protection by fire, cannot be obliterated.

After a time—worn out by a day of nerve-strain and of battling with swift currents, of flight from Something invisible, intangible—they all slept.

The depths of space, star-sprinkled, hung above them with vastness immeasurable, cold beyond all understanding of the human mind.

Jandron woke first, in a red dawn.

He blinked at the fire, as he crawled from his sleeping-bag. The fire was dead; and yet it had not burned out. Much wood remained unconsumed, charred over, as if some gigantic extinguisher had in the night been lowered over it.

"*Hmmm!*" growled Jandron. He glanced about him, on the ledge. "Prints, too. I might have known!"

He aroused Marr. Despite all the journalist's mocking hostility, Jandron felt more in common with this man of his own age than with the Professor, who was close on sixty.

"Look here, now!" said he. "*It* has been all around here. See? *It* put out our fire—maybe the fire annoyed *It*, some way—and *It* walked round us, everywhere." His gray eyes smouldered. "I guess, by gad, you've got to admit facts, now!"

The journalist could only shiver and stare.

"Lord, what a head I've got on me, this morning!" he chattered. He rubbed his forehead with a shaking hand, and started for the river. Most of his assurance had vanished. He looked badly done up.

"Well, what say?" demanded Jandron. "See these fresh prints?"

"Damn the prints!" retorted Marr, and fell to grumbling some unintelligible thing. He washed unsteadily, and remained crouching at the river's lip, inert, numbed.

Jandron, despite a gnawing at the base of his brain, carefully examined the ledge. He found prints scattered everywhere, and some even on the river-bottom near the shore. Wherever water had collected in the prints on the rock, it had frozen hard. Each print in the river-bed, too, was white with ice. Ice that the rushing current could not melt.

"Well, by gad!" he exclaimed. He lighted his pipe and tried to think. Horribly afraid—yes, he felt horribly afraid, but determined. Presently, as a little power of concentration came back, he noticed that all the prints were in straight lines, each mark about two feet from the next.

"*It* was observing us while we slept," said Jandron.

"What nonsense are you talking, eh?" demanded Marr. His dark, heavy face sagged. "Fire, now, and grub!"

He got up and shuffled unsteadily away from the river. Then he stopped with a jerk, staring.

"Look! Look a' that axe!" he gulped, pointing.

Jandron picked up the axe, by the handle, taking good care not to touch the steel. The blade was white-furred with frost. And deep into it, punching out part of the edge, one of the prints was stamped.

"This metal," said he, "is clean gone. It's been absorbed. The Thing doesn't recognize any difference in materials. Water and steel and rock are all the same to It.

"You're crazy!" snarled the journalist. "How could a Thing travel on one leg, hopping along, making marks like that?"

"It could roll, if it was disk-shaped. And—"

A cry from the Professor turned them. Thorburn was stumbling toward them, hands out and tremulous.

"My wife—!" he choked.

Vivian was kneeling beside her sister, frightened, dazed.

"Something's happened!" stammered the Professor. "Here—come here—!"

Mrs. Thorburn was beyond any power of theirs, to help. She was still breathing; but her respirations were stertorous, and a complete paralysis had stricken her. Her eyes, half-open and expressionless, showed pupils startlingly dilated. No resources of the party's drug-kit produced the slightest effect on the woman.

The next half-hour was a confused panic, breaking camp, getting Mrs. Thorburn into a canoe, and leaving that accursed place, with a furious energy of terror that could no longer reason. Up-stream, ever up against the swirl of the current the party fought, driven by horror. With no thought of food or drink, paying no heed to landmarks, lashed forward only by the mad desire to be gone, the three men and the girl flung every ounce of their energy into the paddles. Their panting breath mingled with the sound of swirling eddies. A mist-blurred sun brooded over the northern wilds. Unheeded, hosts of black-flies sang high-pitched keenings all about the fugitives. On either hand the forest waited, watched.

Only after two hours of sweating toil had brought exhaustion did they stop, in the shelter of a cove where black waters circled, foam-flecked. There they found the Professor's wife—she was dead.

Nothing remained to do but bury her. At first Thorburn would not hear of it. Like a madman he insisted that through all hazards he would fetch the body out. But no—impossible. So, after a terrible time, he yielded.

In spite of her grief, Vivian was admirable. She understood what must be done. It was her voice that said the prayers; her hand that—lacking flowers—laid the fir boughs on the cairn. The Professor was dazed past doing anything, saying anything.

Toward mid-afternoon, the party landed again, many miles up-river. Necessity forced them to eat. Firs would not burn. Every time they lighted it, it smouldered and went out with a heavy, greasy smoke. The fugitives ate cold food and drank water, then shoved off in two canoes and once more fled.

In the third canoe, hauled to the edge of the forest, lay all the rock-specimens, data and curios, scientific instruments. The party kept only Marr's diary, a compass, supplies, fire-arms and medicine-kit.

"We can find the things we've left—sometime," said Jandron, noting the place well. "Sometime—after *It* has gone."

"And bring the body out," added Thorburn. Tears, for the first time, wet his eyes. Vivian said nothing. Marr tried to light his pipe. He seemed to forget that nothing, not even tobacco, would burn now.

Vivian and Jandron occupied one canoe. The other carried the Professor and Marr. Thus the power of the two canoes was about the same. They kept well together, up-stream.

The fugitives paddled and portaged with a dumb, desperate energy. Toward evening they struck into what they believed to be the Mamattawan. A mile up this, as the blurred sun faded beyond a wilderness of ominous silence, they camped. Here they made determined efforts to kindle fire. Not even alcohol from the drug-kit would start it. Cold, they mumbled a little food; cold, they huddled into their sleeping-bags, there to lie with darkness leaden on their fear. After a long time, up over a world void of all sound save the river-flow, slid an amber moon notched by the ragged tops of the conifers. Even the wail of a timber-wolf would have come as welcome relief; but no wolf howled.

Silence and night enfolded them. And everywhere they felt that *It* was watching.

Foolishly enough, as a man will do foolish things in a crisis, Jandron laid his revolver outside his sleeping-bag, in easy reach. His thought—blurred by a strange, drawing headache—was:

"If *It* touches Vivian, I'll shoot!"

He realized the complete absurdity of trying to shoot a visitant from interstellar space; from the Fourth Dimension, maybe. But Jandron's ideas seemed tangled. Nothing would come right. He lay there, absorbed in a kind of waking nightmare. Now and then, rising on an elbow, he hearkened; all in vain. Nothing so much as stirred.

His thought drifted to better days, when all had been health, sanity, optimism; when nothing except jealousy of Marr, as concerned Vivian, had troubled him. Days when the sizzle of the frying-pan over friendly coals had made friendly wilderness music; when the wind and the northern star, the whirr of the reel, the whispering vortex of the paddle in clear water had all been things of joy. Yes, and when a certain happy moment had, through some word or look of the girl, seemed to promise his heart's desire. But now—

"Damn it, I'll save *her*, anyhow!" he swore with savage intensity, knowing all the while that what was to be, would be, unmitigably. Do ants, by any waving of antenna, stay the down-crushing foot of man?

Next morning, and the next, no sign of the Thing appeared. Hope revived that possibly It might have flitted away elsewhere; back, perhaps, to outer space. Many were the miles the urging paddles spurned behind. The fugitives calculated that a week more would bring them to the railroad. Fire burned again. Hot food and drink helped, wonderfully. But where were the fish?

"Most extraordinary," all at once said the Professor, at noonday camp. He had become quite rational again. "Do you realize, Jandron, we've seen no traces of life in some time?"

The geologist nodded. Only too clearly he had noted just that, but he had been keeping still about it.

"That's so, too!" chimed in Marr, enjoying the smoke that some incomprehensible turn of events was letting him have. "Not a muskrat or beaver. Not even a squirrel or bird."

"Not so much as a gnat or black-fly!" the Professor added. Jandron suddenly realized that he would have welcomed even those.

That afternoon, Marr fell into a suddenly vile temper. He mumbled curses against the guides, the current, the portages, everything. The Professor seemed more cheerful. Vivian complained of an oppressive headache. Jandron gave her the last of the aspirin tablets; and as he gave them, took her hand in his.

"I'll see *you* through, anyhow," said he, "I don't count, now. Nobody counts, only you!"

She gave him a long, silent look. He saw the sudden glint of tears in her eyes; felt the pressure of her hand, and knew they two had never been so near each other as in that moment under the shadow of the Unknown.

Next day—or it may have been two days later, for none of them could be quite sure about the passage of time— they came to a deserted lumber-camp. Even more than two days might have passed; because now their bacon was all gone, and only coffee, tobacco, beef-cubes and pilot-bread remained. The lack of fish and game had cut alarmingly into the duffle-bag. That day—whatever day it may have been—all four of them suffered terribly from headaches of an odd, ring-shaped kind, as if something circular were being pressed down about their heads. The Professor said it was the sun that made his head ache. Vivian laid it to the wind and the gleam of the swift water, while Marr claimed it was the heat. Jandron wondered at all this, inasmuch as he plainly saw that the river had almost stopped flowing, and the day had become still and overcast.

They dragged their canoes upon a rotting stage of fir-poles and explored the lumber-camp; a mournful place set back in an old "slash," now partly overgrown with scrub poplar, maple and birch. The log buildings, covered with tar-paper partly torn from the pole roofs, were of the usual North Country type. Obviously the place had not been used for years. Even the landing-stage where once logs had been rolled into the stream had sagged to decay.

"I don't quite get the idea of this," Marr exclaimed. "Where did the logs go to? Downstream, of course. But *that* would take 'em to Hudson Bay, and there's no market for spruce timber or pulpwood at Hudson Bay." He pointed down the current.

"You're entirely mistaken," put in the Professor. "Any fool could see this river runs the other way. A log thrown in here would go down toward the St. Lawrence!"

"But then," asked the girl, "why can't we drift back to civilization?" The Professor retorted:

"Just what we *have* been doing, all along! Extraordinary, that I have to explain the obvious!' He walked away in a huff.

"I don't know but he's right, at that," half admitted the journalist. "I've been thinking almost the same thing, myself, the past day or two—that is, ever since the sun shifted."

"What do you mean, shifted?" from Jandron.

"You haven't noticed it?"

"But there's been no sun at all, for at least two days!"

"Hanged if I'll waste time arguing with a lunatic!" Marr growled. He vouchsafed no explanation of what he meant by the sun's having "shifted," but wandered off, grumbling.

"What *are* we going to do?" the girl appealed to Jandron. The sight of her solemn, frightened eyes, of her palm-outward hands and (at last) her very feminine fear, constricted Jandron's heart.

"We're going through, you and I," he answered simply. "We've got to save them from themselves, you and I have."

Their hands met again, and for a moment held. Despite the dead calm, a fir-tip at the edge of the clearing suddenly flicked aside, shrivelled as if frozen. But neither of them saw it.

The fugitives, badly spent, established themselves in the "bar-room" or sleeping-shack of the camp. They wanted to feel a roof over them again, if only a broken one. The traces of men comforted them: a couple of broken peavies, a pair of snowshoes with the thongs all gnawed off, a cracked bit of mirror, a yellowed almanac dated 1899.

Jandron called the Professor's attention to this almanac, but the Professor thrust it aside.

"What do I want of a Canadian census-report?" he demanded, and fell to counting the bunks, over and over again. The big bulge of his forehead, that housed the massive brain of his, was oozing sweat. Marr cursed what he claimed was sunshine through the holes in the roof, though Jandron could see none; claimed the sunshine made his head ache.

"But it's not a bad place," he added. "We can make a blaze in that fireplace and be comfy. I don't like that window, though."

"What window?" asked Jandron. "Where?"

Marr laughed, and ignored him. Jandron turned to Vivian, who had sunk down on the "deacon-seat" and was staring at the stove.

"*Is* there a window here?" he demanded.

"Don't ask me," she whispered. "I—I don't know."

With a very thriving fear in his heart, Jandron peered at her for a moment. He fell to muttering:

"I'm Wallace Jandron. Wallace Jandron, 37 Ware Street, Cambridge, Massachusetts. I'm quite sane. And I'm going to stay so. I'm going to save her! I know perfectly well what I'm doing. And I'm sane. Quite, quite sane!"

After a time of confused and purposeless wrangling, they got a fire going and made coffee. This, and cube bouillon with hardtack, helped considerably. The camp helped, too. A house, even a poor and broken one, is a wonderful barrier against a Thing from—Outside.

Presently darkness folded down. The men smoked, thankful that tobacco still held out. Vivian lay in a bunk that Jandron had piled with spruce boughs for her, and seemed to sleep. The Professor fretted like a child, over the blisters his paddle had made upon his hands. Marr laughed, now and then; though what he might be laughing at was not apparent. Suddenly he broke out:

"After all, what should It want of us?"

"Our brains, of course," the Professor answered, sharply.

"That lets Jandron out," the journalist mocked.

"But," added the Professor, "I can't imagine a Thing callously destroying human beings. And yet—"

He stopped short, with surging memories of his dead wife.

"What was it," Jandron asked, "that destroyed all those people in Valladolid, Spain, that time so many of 'em died in a few minutes after having been touched by an invisible Something that left a slight red mark on each? The newspapers were full of it."

"Piffle!" yawned Marr.

"I tell you," insisted Jandron, "there are forms of life as superior to us as we are to ants. We can't see 'em. No ant ever saw a man. And did any ant ever form the least conception of a man? These Things have left thousands of traces, all over the world. If I had my reference-books—"

"Tell that to the marines!"

"Charles Fort, the greatest authority in the world on unexplained phenomena," persisted Jandron, "gives innumerable cases of happenings that science can't explain, in his 'Book of the Damned.' He claims this earth was once a No-Man's land where all kinds of Things explored and colonized and fought for possession. And he says that now everybody's warned off, except the Owners. I happen to remember a few sentences of his: 'In the past, inhabitants of a host of worlds have dropped here, hopped here, wafted here, sailed, flown, motored, walked here; have come singly, have come in enormous numbers; have visited for hunting, trading, mining. They have been unable to stay here, have made colonies here, have been lost here.'"

"Poor fish, to believe that!" mocked the journalist, while the Professor blinked and rubbed his bulging forehead.

"I do believe it!" insisted Jandron. "The world is covered with relics of dead civilizations that have mysteriously vanished, leaving nothing but their temples and monuments."

"Rubbish!"

"How about Easter Island? How about all the gigantic works there and in a thousand other places!—Peru, Yucatan and so on—which certainly no primitive race ever built?"

"That's thousands of years ago," said Marr, "and I'm sleepy. For heaven's sake, can it!"

"Oh, all right. But *how* explain things, then!"

"What the devil could one of those Things want of our brains?" suddenly put in the Professor. "After all, what?"

"Well, what do we want of lower forms of life? Sometimes food. Again, some product or other. Or just information. Maybe *It* is just experimenting with us, the way we poke an ant-hill. There's always this to remember, that the human brain-tissue is the most highly-organized form of matter in this world."

"Yes," admitted the Professor, "but what—?"

"*It* might want brain-tissue for food, for experimental purposes, for lubricant—how do I know?"

Jandron fancied he was still explaining things; but all at once he found himself waking up in one of the bunks. He felt terribly cold, stiff, sore. A sift of snow lay here and there on the camp floor, where it had fallen through holes in the roof.

"*Vivian!*" he croaked hoarsely. "Thorburn! Marr!"

Nobody answered. There was nobody to answer. Jandron crawled with immense pain out of his bunk, and blinked round with bleary eyes. All of a sudden he saw the Professor, and gulped.

The Professor was lying stiff and straight in another bunk, on his back. His waxen face made a mask of horror.

The open, staring eyes, with pupils immensely dilated, sent Jandron shuddering back. A livid ring marked the forehead, that now sagged inward as if empty.

"Vivian!" croaked Jandron, staggering away from the body. He fumbled to the bunk where the girl had lain. The bunk was quite deserted.

On the stove, in which lay half-charred wood—wood smothered out as if by some noxious gas—still stood the coffee-pot. The liquid in it was frozen solid. Of Vivian and the journalist, no trace remained.

Along one of the sagging beams that supported the roof, Jandron's horror-blasted gaze perceived a straight line of frosted prints, ring-shaped, bitten deep.

"Vivian! Vivian!"

No answer.

Shaking, sick, gray, half-blind with a horror not of this world, Jandron peered slowly around. The duffle-bag and supplies were gone. Nothing was left but that coffee-pot and the revolver at Jandron's hip.

Jandron turned, then. A-stare, his skull feeling empty as a burst drum, he crept lamely to the door and out—out into the snow.

Snow. It came slanting down. From a gray sky it steadily filtered. The trees showed no leaf. Birches, poplars, rock-maples all stood naked. Only the conifers drooped sickly-green. In a little shallow across the river snow lay white on thin ice.

Ice? Snow? Rapt with terror, Jandron stared. Why, then, he must have been unconscious three or four weeks? But how—?

Suddenly, all along the upper branches of trees that edged the clearing, puffs of snow flicked down. The geologist shuffled after two half-obliterated sets of footprints that wavered toward the landing.

His body was leaden. He wheezed, as he reached the river. The light, dim as it was, hurt his eyes. He blinked in a confusion that could just perceive one canoe was gone. He pressed a hand to his head, where an iron band seemed screwed up tight, tighter.

"Vivian! Marr! Halloooo!"

Not even an echo. Silence clamped the world; silence, and a cold that gnawed. Everything had gone a sinister gray.

After a certain time—though time now possessed neither reality nor duration—Jandron dragged himself back to the camp and stumbled in. Heedless of the staring corpse he crumpled down by the stove and tried to think, but his brain had been emptied of power. Everything blent to a gray blur. Snow kept slithering in through the roof.

"Well, why don't you come and get me, Thing?" suddenly snarled Jandron. "Here I am. Damn you, come and get me!"

Voices. Suddenly he heard voices. Yes, somebody was outside, there. Singularly aggrieved, he got up and limped to the door. He squinted out into the gray; saw two figures down by the landing. With numb indifference he recognized the girl and Marr.

"Why should they bother me again?" he nebulously wondered. "Can't they go away and leave me alone?" He felt peevish irritation.

Then, a modicum of reason returning, he sensed that they were arguing. Vivian, beside a canoe freshly dragged from thin ice, was pointing; Marr was gesticulating. All at once Marr snarled, turned from her, plodded with bent back toward the camp.

"But listen!" she called, her rough-knit sweater all powdered with snow. "*That's* the way!" She gestured downstream.

"I'm not going either way!" Marr retorted. "I'm going to stay right here!" He came on, bareheaded. Snow grayed his stubble of beard; but on his head it melted as it fell, as if some fever there had raised the brain-stuff to improbable temperatures. "I'm going to stay right here, all summer." His heavy lids sagged. Puffy and evil, his lips showed a glint of teeth. "Let me alone!"

Vivian lagged after him, kicking up the ash-like snow. With indifference, Jandron watched them. Trivial human creatures!

Suddenly Marr saw him in the doorway and stopped short. He drew his gun; he aimed at Jandron.

"*You* get out!" he mouthed. "Why in————can't you stay dead?"

"Put that gun down, you idiot!" Jandron managed to retort. The girl stopped and seemed to be trying to understand. "We can get away yet, if we all stick together."

"Are you going to get out and leave me alone?" demanded the journalist, holding his gun steadily enough.

Jandron, wholly indifferent, watched the muzzle. Vague curiosity possessed him. Just what, he wondered, did it feel like to be shot?

Marr pulled the trigger.

Snap!

The cartridge missed fire. Not even powder would burn.

Marr laughed, horribly, and shambled forward. "Serves him right!" he mouthed. "He'd better not come back again!"

Jandron understood that Marr had seen him fall. But still he felt himself standing there, alive. He shuffled away from the door. No matter whether he was alive or dead, there was always Vivian to be saved.

The journalist came to the door, paused, looked down, grunted and passed into the camp. He shut the door. Jandron heard the rotten wooden bar of the latch drop. From within echoed a laugh, monstrous in its brutality.

Then quivering, the geologist felt a touch on his arm.

"Why did you desert us like that?" he heard Vivian's reproach. "Why?"

He turned, hardly able to see her at all.

"Listen," he said, thickly. "I'll admit anything. It's all right. But just forget it, for now. We've got to get out o' here. The Professor is dead in there, and Marr's gone mad and barricaded himself in there. So there's no use staying. There's a chance for us yet. Come along!"

He took her by the arm and tried to draw her toward the river, but she held back. The hate in her face sickened him. He shook in the grip of a mighty chill.

"Go, with—you?" she demanded.

"Yes, by God!" he retorted, in a swift blaze of anger, "or I'll kill you where you stand. *It* shan't get you, anyhow!"

Swiftly piercing, a greater cold smote to his inner marrows. A long row of the cup-shaped prints had just appeared in the snow beside the camp. And from these marks wafted a faint, bluish vapor of unthinkable cold.

"What are you staring at?" the girl demanded.

"Those prints! In the snow, there—see?" He pointed a shaking finger.

"How can there be snow at this season?"

He could have wept for the pity of her, the love of her. On her red tam, her tangle of rebel hair, her sweater, the snow came steadily drifting; yet there she stood before him and prated of summer. Jandron heaved himself out of a very slough of down-dragging lassitudes. He whipped himself into action.

"Summer, winter—no matter!" he flung at her. "You're coming along with me!" He seized her arm with the brutality of desperation that must hurt, to save. And murder, too, lay in his soul. He knew that he would strangle her with his naked hands, if need were, before he would ever leave her there, for It to work Its horrible will upon.

"You come with me," he mouthed, "or by the Almighty—!"

Marr's scream in the camp, whirled him toward the door. That scream rose higher, higher, even more and more piercing, just like the screams of the runaway Indian guides in what now appeared the infinitely long ago. It seemed to last hours; and always it rose, rose, as if being wrung out of a human body by some kind of agony not conceivable in this world. Higher, higher—

Then it stopped.

Jandron hurled himself against the plank door. The bar smashed; the door shivered inward.

With a cry, Jandron recoiled. He covered his eyes with a hand that quivered, claw-like.

"Go away, Vivian! Don't come here—don't look—"

He stumbled away, babbling.

Out of the door crept something like a man. A queer, broken, bent over thing; a thing crippled, shrunken and flabby, that whined.

This thing—yes, it was still Marr—crouched down at one side, quivering, whimpering. It moved its hands as a crushed ant moves its antennæ, jerkily, without significance.

All at once Jandron no longer felt afraid. He walked quite steadily to Marr, who was breathing in little gasps. From the camp issued an odor unlike anything terrestrial. A thin, grayish grease covered the sill.

Jandron caught hold of the crumpling journalist's arm. Marr's eyes leered, filmed, unseeing. He gave the impression of a creature whose back has been broken, whose whole essence and energy have been wrenched asunder, yet in which life somehow clings, palpitant. A creature vivisected.

Away through the snow Jandron dragged him. Marr made no resistance; just let himself be led, whining a little, palsied, rickety, shattered. The girl, her face whitely cold as the snow that fell on it, came after.

Thus they reached the landing at the river.

"Come, now, let's get away!" Jandron made shift to articulate. Marr said nothing. But when Jandron tried to bundle him into a canoe, something in the journalist revived with swift, mad hatefulness. That something lashed him into a spasm of wiry, incredibly venomous resistance. Slavers of blood and foam streaked Marr's lips. He made horrid noises, like an animal. He howled dismally, and bit, clawed, writhed and grovelled! He tried to sink his teeth into Jandron's leg. He fought appallingly, as men must have fought in the inconceivably remote days even before the Stone Age. And Vivian helped him. Her fury was a tiger-cat's.

Between the pair of them, they almost did him in. They almost dragged Jandron down—and themselves, too—into the black river that ran swiftly sucking under the ice. Not till Jandron had quite flung off all vague notions and restraints of gallantry; not until he struck from the shoulder—to kill, if need were—did he best them.

He beat the pair of them unconscious, trussed them hand and foot with the painters of the canoes, rolled them into the larger canoe, and shoved off. After that, the blankness of a measureless oblivion descended.

Only from what he was told, weeks after, in the Royal Victoria Hospital at Montreal, did Jandron ever learn how and when a field-squad of Dominion Foresters had found them drifting in Lake Moosawamkeag. And that knowledge filtered slowly into his brain during a period inchoate as Iceland fogs.

That Marr was dead and the girl alive—that much, at all events, was solid. He could hold to that; he could climb back, with that, to the real world again.

Jandron climbed back, came back. Time healed him, as it healed the girl. After a long, long while, they had speech together. Cautiously he sounded her wells of memory. He saw that she recalled nothing. So he told her white lies about capsized canoes and the sad death—in realistically-described rapids—of all the party except herself and him.

Vivian believed. Fate, Jandron knew, was being very kind to both of them.

But Vivian could never understand in the least why her husband, not very long after marriage, asked her not to wear a wedding-ring or any ring whatsoever.

"Men are so queer!" covers a multitude of psychic agonies.

Life, for Jandron—life, softened by Vivian—knit itself up into some reasonable semblance of a normal pattern. But when, at lengthening intervals, memories even now awake—memories crawling amid the slime of cosmic mysteries that it is madness to approach—or when at certain times Jandron sees a ring of any sort, his heart chills with a cold that reeks of the horrors of Infinity.

And from shadows past the boundaries of our universe seem to beckon Things that, God grant, can never till the end of time be known on earth.

1923

THE FINDING OF THE ABSOLUTE

May Sinclair

I.

Mr. Spalding had gone out into the garden to find peace, and had not found it. He sat there, with hunched shoulders and bowed head, dejected in the spring sunshine.

Jerry, the black cat, invited him to play; he stood on his hind legs and danced, and bowed sideways, and waved his forelegs in the air like wings. At any other time his behaviour would have enchanted Mr. Spalding, but now he couldn't even look at him; he was too miserable.

He had gone to bed miserable; he had passed a night of misery, and he had waked up more miserable than ever. He had been like that for three days and three nights straight on end, and no wonder. It wasn't only that his young wife Elizabeth had run away with Paul Jeffreson, the Imagist poet. Besides the frailty of Elizabeth, he had discovered a fatal flaw in his own system of metaphysics. His belief in Elizabeth was gone. So was his belief in the Absolute.

The two things had come at once, to crush him. And he had to own bitterly that they were not altogether unrelated. "If," Mr. Spalding said to himself, "I had served my wife as faithfully as I have served my God, she would not now have deserted me for Paul Jeffreson." He meant that if he had not been wrapped up in his system of metaphysics,

Elizabeth might still have been wrapped up in him. He had nobody but himself to thank for her behaviour.

If she had run away with anybody else, since run she must, he might have forgiven her; he might have forgiven himself; but there could be nothing but misery in store for Elizabeth. Paul Jeffreson had genius, Mr. Spalding didn't deny it; immortal genius; but he had no morals; he drank; he drugged; in Mr. Spalding's decent phrase, he did everything he shouldn't do.

You would have thought this overwhelming disaster would have completely outweighed the other trouble. But no; Mr. Spalding had a balanced mind; he mourned with equal sorrow the loss of his wife and the loss of his Absolute. A flaw in a metaphysical system may seem to you a small thing; but you must bear in mind that, ever since he could think at all, Mr. Spalding had been devoured by a hunger and thirst after metaphysical truth. He had flung over the God he had been taught to believe in because, besides being an outrage to Mr. Spalding's moral sense, he wasn't metaphysical enough. The poor man was always worrying about metaphysics; he wandered from system to system, seeking truth, seeking reality, seeking some supreme intellectual satisfaction that never came. He thought he had found it in his theory of Absolute Pantheism. But really, Spalding's Pantheism, anybody's Pantheism for that matter, couldn't, when you brought it down to bed-rock thinking, hold water for a minute. And the more Absolute he made it, the leakier it was.

For, consider, on Mr. Spalding's theory, there isn't any reality except the Absolute. Things are only real because they exist in It; because It is Them. Mr. Spalding conceived that his consciousness and Elizabeth's consciousness and Paul Jeffreson's consciousness existed somehow in the Absolute unchanged. For, if that inside existence changed them you would have to say that the ground of their present appearance lay somewhere outside the Absolute, which to Mr. Spalding was rank blasphemy. And if Elizabeth and Paul Jeffreson existed in the Absolute unchanged, then their adultery existed there unchanged. And an adultery within the Absolute outraged his moral sense as much as anything he had been told about God in his youth. The odd thing was that until Elizabeth had run away and committed it he had never thought of that. The metaphysics of Pantheism had interested him much more than its ethics. And now he could think of nothing else.

And it wasn't only Elizabeth and her iniquity; there were all the intolerable people he had ever known. There was his Uncle Sims, a mean sneak if ever there was one; and his Aunt Emily, a silly fool; and his cousin, Tom Rumbold, an obscene idiot. And his uncle's mean sneak-ishness, and his aunt's silly folly, and his cousin's obscene idiocy would have to exist in the Absolute, too; and unchanged, mind you.

And the things you see and hear—A blue sky, now, would it be blue in the Sight of God, or just something inconceivable? And noises, music? For example, I am listening to Grand Opera, and you to the jazz band in your restaurant; but the God of Pantheism is listening to both, to all the noises in the universe at once. As if He had sat down on the piano. This idea shocked Mr. Spalding even more than the thought of Elizabeth's misconduct.

Time went on. Paul Jeffreson drank himself to death. Elizabeth, worn out with grief, died of pneumonia following influenza; and Mr. Spalding still went about worrying over his inadjustable metaphysics.

And at last he, too, found himself dying.

And then he began to worry about other things. Things that had, as he put it, "happened" in his youth, before he knew Elizabeth, and one thing that had happened after she left him. He thought of them as just happening; happening *to* him rather than *through* him, against his will. In calm, philosophic moments he couldn't conceive how they had ever happened at all, how, for example, he could have endured Connie Larkins. The episodes had been brief, because in each case boredom and disgust had supervened to put asunder what Mr. Spalding owned should never have been joined. Brief, insignificant as they were, Mr. Spalding, in his dying state, was worried when he looked back on them. Supposing they were more significant than they had seemed? Supposing they had an eternal significance and entailed tremendous consequences in the after-life? Supposing you were not just wiped out, that there really *was* an after-life? Supposing that in that other world there was a hell?

Mr. Spalding could imagine no worse hell than the eternal repetition of such incidents; eternal repetition of boredom and disgust. Fancy going on with Connie Larkins for ever and ever, never being able to get away from her, doomed to repeat—And, if there *was* an Absolute, if there was reality, truth, never knowing it; being cut off from it for ever—

"He that is filthy let him be filthy still."

That was hell, the continuance of the filthy state.

He wondered whether goodness was not, after all, *the* important thing; he wondered whether there really was a next world; with an extreme uneasiness he wondered what would happen to him in it.

He died wondering.

II.

His first thought was: Well, here I am again. I've not been wiped out. His next, that he hadn't died at all. He had gone to sleep and was now dreaming. He was not in the least agitated, nor even surprised.

He found himself alone in an immense grey space, in which there was no distinguishable object but himself. He was aware of his body as occupying a portion of this space. For he had a body; a curious, tenuous, whitish body. The odd thing was that this empty space had a sort of solidity under him. He was lying on it, stretched out on it, adrift. It supported him with the buoyancy of deep water. And yet his body was part of it, netted in.

He was now aware of two figures approaching. They came and stood, like figures treading water, one on each side of him, and he saw that they were Elizabeth and Paul Jeffreson.

Then he concluded that he was really dead; dead like Elizabeth and Jeffreson, and (since they were there) that he was in hell.

Elizabeth was speaking, and her voice sounded sweet and very kind. All the same he knew he was in hell.

"It's all right," she said. "It's queer at first, but you'll get used to it. You don't mind our coming to meet you?"

Mr. Spalding said he'd no business to mind, no right to reproach her, since they were all in the same boat. They had, all three, deserved their punishment.

"Punishment?" (Jeffreson spoke). "Why, where does he think he is?"

"I'm in hell, aren't I? If—"

"If *we're* here. Is that it?"

"Well, Jeffreson, I don't want to rake up old unpleasantness, but after—after what happened, you'll forgive my saying so, but what else *can* I think?"

He heard Jeffreson laugh; a perfectly natural laugh.

"Will *you* tell him, Elizabeth, or shall I?"

"You'd better. He always respected your intelligence."

"Well, old chap, if you really want to know where you are, you're in heaven."

"You don't mean to say so?"

"Fact. I daresay you're wondering what we're doing here?"

"Well, Elizabeth—perhaps. But, frankly, Jeffreson . . ."

"Yes. How about me?"

"With your record I should have thought you'd even less business here than I have."

"Wouldn't you? I lived on unpaid bills. I drank. I drugged. There was nothing I didn't do. What do you suppose I got in on? You'll never guess."

"No. No. I give it up."

May Sinclair

"My love of beauty. You wouldn't think it, but it seems that actually counts here, in the eternal world."

"And Elizabeth, what did she get in on?"

"Her love of me."

"Then all I can say is," said Mr. Spalding, "Heaven must be a most immoral place."

"Oh, no. Your parochial morality doesn't hold good here, that's all. Why should it? It's entirely relative. Relative to a social system with limits in time and space. Relative to a certain biological configuration that ceased with our terrestrial organisms. Not absolute. Not eternal.

"But beauty—Beauty *is* eternal, is absolute. And I—I loved beauty more than credit, more than drink or drugs or women, more even than Elizabeth.

"And love is eternal. And Elizabeth loved me more than you, more than respectability, more than peace and comfort, and a happy life."

"That's all very well, Jeffreson; and Elizabeth may be all right. Mary Magdalene, you know. *Quia mulium amavit*, and so forth. But if a blackguard like you can slip into heaven as easily as all that, where *are* our ethics?"

"Your ethics, my dear Spalding, are where they've always been, where you came from, not here. And if I *was* what they call a bad man, that's to say a bad terrestrial organism, I was a thundering good poet. You say I slipped in easily; do you suppose it's easy to be a poet? My dear fellow, it requires an inflexibility, a purity, a discipline of mind—of *mind*, remember—that you haven't any conception of. And surely *you* should be the last person in the world to regard mind as an inferior secondary affair.

Anyhow, the consequence is that I've not only got into heaven, I've got into one of the best heavens, a heaven reserved exclusively for the very finest spirits."

"Then," said Mr. Spalding, "if we're in heaven, who's in hell?"

"Couldn't say for certain. But we shouldn't put it that way. We should say: Who's gone back to earth?"

"Well—am I likely to meet Uncle Sims, or Aunt Emily, or Tom Rumbold here? You remember them, Elizabeth?"

"Oh, yes, I remember. They'd be almost certain to be sent back. They couldn't stand eternal things. There's nothing eternal about meanness and stupidity and nastiness."

"What'll happen to them, do you suppose?"

"What should you say, Paul?"

"I should say they'd suffer damnably till they'd got some bigness and intelligence and decency knocked into them."

"It'll be a sell for Aunt Emily. She was brought up to believe that stupidity was no drawback to getting into heaven."

"Lots of people," said Jeffreson, "will be sold. Like my father, the Dean of Eastminster; he was cocksure he'd get in; but they won't let him. And why, do you suppose? Because the poor old boy couldn't see that my poems were beautiful.

"But even that wouldn't have dished him, if he'd had a passion for anybody; or if he'd cared two straws about metaphysical truth. Your truth, Spalding."

"Bless me, all our preconceived ideas seem to have been wrong."

"Yes. Even I wasn't prepared for that. By the way, that's what you got in on, your passion for truth. It's like my passion for beauty."

"But—aren't you distressed about your father, Jeffreson?"

"Oh, no. He'll get into some heaven or other some day. He'll find out that he cares for somebody, perhaps. Then he'll be all right—But don't you want to look about a bit?"

"I don't see very much to look at. It strikes me as a bit bare, your heaven."

"Oh, that's because you're only at the landing-state."

"The landing *what*?"

"State. What we used to call landing place. Times and spaces here, you know, are states. States of mind."

Mr. Spalding sat up, excited. "But—but that's what I always said they were. I and Kant."

"Well, you'd better talk to him about it."

"Talk to *him*? Shall I see Kant?"

"Look at him, Elizabeth. *Now* he's coming alive—Of course you'll see him when you get into your own place— state, I mean. You'd better get up and come along with me and Elizabeth. We'll show you round."

He rose, they steadied him, and he made his way between them through the grey immensity, over a half-seen yet perfectly solid tract of something that he thought of, absurdly, as condensed space. As yet there were no objects in sight but the figures of Elizabeth and Jeffreson; the half-seen, yet tangible floor he went on seemed to create itself out of nothing, under his feet, as the desire to walk arose in him. And as yet he had felt no interest or curiosity; but as he went on he was aware of a desire to see things that became more and more urgent. He would see. He must see. He felt that before him and around him there were endless things to be seen. His mind strained forwards towards vision.

And then, suddenly, he saw.

He saw a landscape more beautiful than anything he could have imagined. It was, Jeffreson informed him, very like the umbrella pine country between Florence and Siena. As they came out of it on a great, curving road they had their faces towards the celestial west. To the south the land fell away in great red cliffs to a shining, blue sea. Like, Jeffreson said, the Riviera, the Estérel. West and north the landscape rolled in green hill after green hill, pine-tufted, to a sweeping rampart of deep blue; such a rampart, such blue as Mr. Spalding had seen from the heights above Sidmouth, looking towards Dartmoor. Only this country had a grace, a harmony of line and colour that gave it an absolute beauty; and over it there lay a serene, unearthly radiance.

Before them, on a hill, was an exquisite little white, golden and rose-red town.

"You may or may not believe me," said Jeffreson, "but the beauty of all this is that I made it. I mean Elizabeth and I made it between us."

"You made it?"

"Made it."

"How?"

"By thinking of it. By wanting it. By imagining it."

"But—out of what?"

"I don't know and I don't much care. Our scientists here will tell you we made it out of the ultimate constituents of matter. Matter, unformed, only exists for us in its ultimate constituents. Something like electrons of electrons of electrons. Here we are all suspended in a web, immersed, if you like, in a sea, an air of this matter. It is utterly plastic to our imagination and our will. Imperceptible in its unformed state, it becomes visible and tangible as our minds get to work on it, and we can make out of it anything we want, including our own bodies. Only, so far as our imaginations are still under the dominion of our memories, so far will the things they create resemble the things we knew on earth. Thus you will notice that while Elizabeth and I are much more beautiful than we were on earth" (he *had* noticed it), "because we desired to be more beautiful, we are still recognizable as Paul and Elizabeth because our imaginations are controlled by our memories. You are as you always were, only younger than when we knew you, because your imagination had nothing but memory to go on. Everything you create here will probably be a replica of something on earth you remember."

"But if I want something new, something beautiful that I haven't seen before, can't I have it?"

"Of course you can have it. Only, just at first, until your own imagination develops, you'll have to come to me or Turner or Michael Angelo to make it for you."

"And will these things that you and Turner and Michael Angelo make for me be permanent?"

"Absolutely, unless we unmade them. And I don't think we should do that against your will. Anyhow, though we can destroy our own works we can't destroy each other's, that is to say, reduce them to their ultimate constituents. What's more, we shouldn't dream of trying."

"Why not?"

"Because old motives don't work here. Envy, greed, theft, robbery, murder, or any sort of destruction, are unknown. They can't happen. Nothing alters matter here but mind, and I can't will your body to come to pieces so long as you want it to keep together. You can't destroy it yourself as you can other things you make, because your need of it is greater than your need of other things.

"We can't thieve or rob for the same reason. Things that belong to us belong to our state of mind and can't be torn away from it, so that we couldn't remove anything from another person's state into our own. And if we could we shouldn't want to, because each of us can always have everything he wants. If I like your house or your landscape better than my own, I can make one for myself just like it. But we don't do this, because we're proud of our individualities here, and would rather have things different than the same—By the way, as you haven't got a house yet, let alone a landscape, you'd better share ours."

"That's very good of you," Mr. Spalding said. He was thinking of Oxford. Oxford. Quiet rooms in Balliol. He seemed to hesitate.

"If you're still sitting on that old grievance of yours, I tell you, once for all, Spalding, I'm not going to express any regret. I'm *not* sorry, I'm glad I took Elizabeth away from you. I made her more happy than unhappy even on

May Sinclair

earth. And please notice it's I who got her into heaven, not you. If she'd stayed with you and hated you, as she would have done, she couldn't have got in."

"I wasn't thinking of that," said Mr. Spalding. "I was only wondering where I could put my landscape."

"How do you mean—'put' it?"

"Place it—so as not to interfere with other people's landscapes."

"But how on earth could you interfere? You 'place' it, as you call it, in your own space and in your own time." His own space, his own time—Mr. Spalding got more and more excited.

"But—how?"

"Oh, I can't tell you how. It simply happens."

"But I want to understand it. I—I *must* understand."

"You shouldn't put him off like that, Paul," Elizabeth said. "He always did want to understand things."

"But when I don't understand them myself—"

"You'd better take him to Kant, or Hegel."

"I should prefer Kant," said Mr. Spalding.

"Well, Kant then. You'll have to get into his state first."

"How do I do that?"

"It's very simple. You just think him up and ask him if you can come in."

Elizabeth explained. "Like ringing somebody up, you know, and asking if you can come and call."

"Supposing he won't let me."

"Trust him to say so. Of course, we mayn't get through. He may have *thought off*."

"You can think off, can you?"

"Yes, that's how you protect yourself. Otherwise life here would be unbearable. Just keep quiet for a second, will you?"

There was an intense silence. Presently Jeffreson said: "Now you're through."

And Mr. Spalding found himself in a white-washed room, scantily furnished with three rows of bookshelves, a writing-table, a table set with mysterious instruments, and two chairs. A shaded lamp on the writing-table gave light. Mr. Spalding had left the umbrella pine country blazing with sunlight, but it seemed that Kant's time was somewhere about ten o'clock at night. The large window was bared to a dark-blue sky of stars.

A little, middle-aged man sat at the writing-table. He wore eighteenth-century clothes and a tie wig. The face that looked up at Mr. Spalding was lean and dried, the mouth tight, the eyes shining distantly with a deep, indrawn intelligence. Mr. Spalding understood that he was in the presence of Immanuel Kant.

"You thought me up?"

"Forgive me. I am James Spalding, a student of philosophy. I was told that you might, perhaps, be willing to explain to me the—the very extraordinary conditions in which I find myself."

"May I ask, Mr. Spalding, if you have paid any particular attention to *my* philosophy?"

"I am one of your most devoted disciples, sir. I refuse to believe that philosophy has made any considerable advance since the Critique of Pure Reason."

"T-t-t. My successor, Hegel, made a very considerable advance. If you have neglected Hegel—"

"Pardon me, I have not. I was once Hegel's devoted disciple. An entrancing fantasy, the Triple Dialectic. But I came to see that yours, sir, was the safer and the saner system, and that the recurrent tendency of philosophy must be back to Kant."

"Better say Forward with him. If you are indeed my disciple, I do not think that conditions here should have struck you as extraordinary."

"They struck me as an extraordinary confirmation of your theory of space and time, sir."

"They are that. They are that. But they go far beyond anything I ever dreamed of. It was not in my scheme that the Will—to which, if you remember, I gave a purely ethical and pragmatical rôle—that the Will and the imagination of individuals, of you and me, Mr. Spalding, should create their own space and time, and their own objects in space and time. I did not anticipate this multiplicity of spaces and times. In my time there was only one space and one time for everybody.

"Still, it is a very remarkable confirmation, and you may imagine, Mr. Spalding, that I was gratified when I first came here to find everybody talking and thinking correctly about time and space. You will have noticed that here we say state, meaning state of consciousness, where we used to say place. In the same way we talk about states of time, meaning time as a state of consciousness. My present state, you will observe, is exactly ten minutes past ten by my clock, which is my consciousness. My consciousness registers time automatically. My own time, mind you, not other people's."

"But isn't that frightfully inconvenient? If your time isn't everybody else's time, how on earth—I mean how in heaven—do you keep your appointments? How do you co-ordinate?"

"We keep appointments, we co-ordinate, exactly as we used to do, by a purely arbitrary system. We measure time by space, by events, movements in space-time. Only, whereas under earthly conditions there was apparently one earth and one sun, one day and one night for everybody, here everybody has his own earth, his own sun and his own day and night. So we are obliged to take an ideal earth and sun, an ideal day and night. Their revolutions are measured exactly as we measured them on earth, by the movements of hands on a dial marking minutes and hours. Only our public clocks have five hands marking the revolutions of weeks, months and years. That is our public standardized time, and all appointments are kept, all scientific calculations made by it. The only difference between heaven and earth is that here public space-time is regarded as it really is—an unreal, a purely arbitrary and artificial convention. We know, not as a result of philosophic or mathematical reasoning, but as part of our ordinary conscious experience, that there is no absolute space and no absolute time. I would say no *real* space and no real time, but that in heaven a state of consciousness carries its own reality with it as such; and the time state or the space state is as real as any other.

"Of course, without an arbitrary public space-time, a public clock, states of consciousness from individual to individual could never be co-ordinated. For example, you have come straight from Mr. Jeffreson's twelve-noon to my ten o'clock p.m. But the public clock, which you will see out there in the street—we are in Königsberg; I have no visual imagination and must rely entirely on memory for my scenery—the public dock, I say, marks time at a quarter to eight; and if I were asking Mr. Jeffreson to spend the evening with me, the hour would be fixed for us by public time at eight. But he would find himself in my time at ten.

"Now I want to point out to you, Mr. Spalding, that this way of regarding space and time is not so revolutionary as it may appear. I said, if you remember, that under terrestrial conditions there was apparently one earth and one sun, one day and night for everybody. But really, even then, everybody carried about with him his own private space and time, and his own private world in space and time. It was only, even then, by an arbitrary system of mathematical conventions, mostly geometrical, that all these private times and spaces were co-ordinated, so as to constitute one universe. Public clock time, based on the revolutions of bodies in a mathematically determined public space, was as conventional and relative an affair on earth as it is in heaven.

"Our private consciousnesses registered their own times automatically then as now, by the passage of internal events. If events passed quickly, our private time outran clock time; if they dragged, it was behindhand.

"Thus in dream experience there are many more events to the second than in waking experience; and consciousness registers by the tick-tick of events, so that in a dream we may live through crowded hours and days in the fraction of time that coincides with the knock on the door that waked us. It is absurd to say that in this case we do not live in two different time-systems."

"Yes, and—" Mr. Spalding cried out excitedly—

"Einstein has proved that motion in public space-time is a purely relative and arbitrary thing, and that the velocity, or time value, of a ray of light moving under different conditions is a constant; when on any theory of absolute time and absolute motion it should be a variant."

"That," said Kant, "is no more than I should have expected."

"You said, sir, that the only distinction between earthly and heavenly conditions is that this artificial character of standardized space-time is recognized in heaven and not on earth. I should have said that the most striking differences were, firstly, that in heaven our experience is created for us by our imagination and our will, whereas on earth it was, in your own word, sir, 'given.' Secondly that in heaven our states are not closed as they were on earth, but that anybody can enter anybody else's. It seems to me that these differences are so great as to surpass anything in our experience on earth."

"They are not so great," said Kant, "as all that. In dreaming you already had an experience of a world created by each person for himself in a space and time of his own; a world in which you transcended the conditions of ordinary space and time. In telepathy and clairvoyance you had experience of entering other people's states."

"But," Mr. Spalding said, "on earth my consciousness was dependent on a world apparently outside it, arising presumably in God's consciousness, my body being the ostensible medium. Here, on the contrary, I have my world inside me, created by my consciousness, and my body is not so much a medium as an accessory after the fact."

"And what inference do you draw, Mr. Spalding?"

"Why, that on earth I was nearer God, more dependent on him than in heaven. I seem to have become my own God."

"Doesn't it strike you that in becoming more god-like you are actually nearer God? That in this power of your imagination to conceive, this freedom of your will to create your universe, God is cutting a clearer path for himself than through that constrained and obstructed consciousness you had on earth?"

"That's it. When I think of that appalling life of earth, the pain, sir, the horrible pain, the wickedness, the imbecility, the endless struggling through blood and filth, and being beaten, I can't help wondering how such things can exist in the Absolute, and why the Absolute shouldn't have put us—or as you would say, *thought* us into this heavenly state from the beginning."

"Do you suppose that any finite intelligence—any finite will could have been trusted, untrained, with the power we have here? Only wills disciplined by struggling against earth's evil, only intelligences braced by wrestling with earth's problems are fitted to create universes. You may remember my enthusiasm for the moral law, my Categorical Imperative? It is not diminished. The moral law still holds and always will hold on earth. But I see now it is not an end in itself, only the means to which this power, this freedom is the end.

"That is how and why pain and evil exist in the Absolute. It is obvious that they cannot exist in it as such, being purely relative to states of terrestrial organisms. That is why the comparatively free wills of terrestrial organisms are permitted to create pain and evil.

"When you talk of such things existing in the Absolute, unchanged and unabridged, you are talking nonsense. You are thinking of pain and evil in terms of one dimension of time and three dimensions of space, by which they are indefinitely multiplied."

"How do you mean—one dimension of time?"

"I mean time taken as linear extension, the pure succession of past, present and future. You think of pain and evil as indefinitely distributed in space and indefinitely repeated in time, whereas in the idea, which is their form of eternity, at their worst they are not many, but one."

"That doesn't make them less unbearable,"

"I am not talking about that. I am talking about their significance for eternity, or in the Absolute, since you said that was what distressed you.

"You will see this for yourself if you will come with me into the state of three dimensional time."

"What's that?" said Mr. Spalding, deeply intrigued. "That," said the philosopher, "is time which is not linear succession, time which has turned on itself twice to take up the past and future into its present. For as the point is repeated to form the line of space, so the instant is repeated to form the linear time of past, present, future. And as the one-dimensional line turns at right angles to itself to form the two-dimensional plane, so linear or one-dimensional time turns on itself to form two-dimensional or plane time, the past-present, or present-future. And as the plane turns on itself to form the cube, so past-present and present-future double back to meet each other and form cubic time, or past-present-future all together.

"This is the three dimensional state of consciousness we shall have to think ourselves into."

"Do you mean to say that if we get into it we shall have solved the riddle of the universe?"

"Hardly. The universe is a tremendous jig-saw puzzle. If God wanted to keep us amused to all eternity, he couldn't have hit on anything better. We shall not be able to stay very long, or to take in *all* past-present-future at once. But you will see enough to realize what cubic time is. You will begin with one small cubic section, which will gradually enlarge until you have taken in as much cubic time as you can hold together in one duration.

"Look out through that window. You see that cart coming down the street. It will have to pass Herr Schmidt's house opposite and the 'Prussian Soldier,' and that grocer's shop and the clock before it gets to the church.

"Now you'll see what'll happen."

III.

What Mr. Spalding saw was the sudden stoppage of the cart, which now appeared as standing simultaneously at each station, Herr Schmidt's house, the inn, the grocery, the clock, the church and the side street up which it had not yet turned.

In this vision solid objects became transparent, so that he saw the side street through the intervening houses. In the same way, distributed in space as on a Mercator's projection, he saw all the subsequent stations of the cart, up to its arrival in a farmyard between a stable and a haystack. In the same duration of time, which was his present, he saw the townspeople moving in their houses, eating, smoking and going to bed, and the peasants in their farms and cottages, and the household of the Graf in his castle. These figures retained all their positions while the amazing experience lasted.

The scene widened. It became all Königsberg, and Königsberg became all Prussia, and Prussia all Europe. Mr. Spalding seemed to have eyes at the sides and back of his head. He saw time rising up round him as an immense cubic space. He was aware of the French Revolution, the Napoleonic wars, the Franco-Prussian war, the establishment of the French Republic, the Boer war, the death of Queen Victoria, the accession and death of King Edward VII., the accession of King George V., the Great War, the Russian and German Revolutions, the rise of the Irish Republic, the Indian Republic, the British Revolution, the British Republic, the conquest of Japan by America, and the federation of the United States of Europe and America, all going on at once.

The scene stretched and stretched, and still Mr. Spalding kept before him every item as it had first appeared. He was now aware of the vast periods of geologic time. On the past side he saw the mammoth and the caveman; on the future he saw the Atlantic flooding the North Sea and submerging the flats of Lincolnshire, Cambridgeshire, Norfolk, Suffolk, Essex, and Kent. He saw the giant tree-ferns; he saw the great saurians trampling the marshlands and sea-beaches of the past. A flight of fearful pterodactyls darkened the air. And he saw the ice creep down and down from the poles to the vast temperate zone of Europe, America and Australasia; he saw men and animals driven before it to the belt of the equator.

And now he sank down deeper; he was swept into the stream that flowed, thudding and throbbing, through all live things; he felt it beat in and around him, jet after jet from the beating heart of God; he felt the rising of the sap in trees, the delight of animals at mating-time. He knew the joy that made Jerry, the black cat, dance on his hind legs and bow sideways and wave his forelegs like wings. The stars whirled past him with a noise like violin strings, and through it he heard the voice of Paul Jeffreson, singing a song. He was aware of an immense, all-pervading rapture pierced with stabs of pain. At the same time he was drawn back on the ebb of life into a curious peace.

His stretch widened. He was present at the beginning and the end. He saw the earth flung off, an incandescent ball, from the wheeling sun. He saw it hang like a dead white moon in a sky strewn with the corpses of spent worlds. But to his surprise he saw no darkness. He learned that light is older than the suns; that they are born of it, not it of them. The whole universe stood up on end round him, doubling all its future back upon all its past.

He saw the vast planes of time intersecting each other, like the planes of a sphere, wheeling, turning in and out of each other. He saw other space and time systems rising up, toppling, enclosing and enclosed. And as a tiny inset in the immense scene, his own life from birth to the present moment, together with the events of his heavenly life to come. In this vision Elizabeth's adultery, which had once appeared so monstrous, so overpowering an event, was revealed as slender and insignificant.

And now the universe dissolved into the ultimate constituents of matter, electrons of electrons of electrons, an unseen web, intensely vibrating, stretched through all space and all time. He saw it sucked back into the space of space, the time of time, into the thought of God.

Mr. Spalding was drawn in with it. He passed from God's immanent to his transcendent life, into the Absolute. For one moment he thought that this was death; the next his whole being swelled and went on swelling in an unspeakable, an unthinkable bliss.

Joined with him, vibrating with him in one tremendous rapture, were the spirits of Elizabeth and Paul Jeffreson. He had now no memory of their adultery or of his own.

When he came out of his ecstasy he was aware that God was spinning his thought again, stretching the web of matter through space and time.

He was going to make another jig-saw puzzle of a universe.

1923

THE VEILED FEMINISTS OF ATLANTIS

Booth Tarkington

Among certain occultists of the esoteric Buddhist group there was once this tradition concerned with the sinking of Atlantis. The continent disappeared as the climax of a conflict between the practitioners of White Magic and those who were experts in Black Magic. Magic, which was of course only science kept secret, had gone far in Atlantis, and the magicians ruled the continent. The general populace was morally unfit to be trusted with knowledge of the discoveries made by initiated chemists, psychologists, electricians, and biologists, just as a portion of our people to-day are unfit to be trusted with automobiles and gunpowder; and therefore the Atlantean scientists were an organized secret society, keeping their knowledge strictly to themselves and using it for the general good. Of course they easily became the ruling class, and the government was naturally a dictatorship, probably a hidden one, so that the populace believed itself to be a governing democracy.

Apprentices to the magicians were carefully selected; only young men of promising intelligence combined with the highest sense of honor and the most humanitarian impulses could be permitted to acquire knowledge potentially dangerous, but mistakes were made in selection; ambitious and prying outsiders obtained copies of some of the sacred books, deciphering them and possessing their meanings; there arose factions, too; and, moreover, some of the greatest among the magicians, or scientists, could not control their own human impulses, and used their knowledge for selfish ends. Thus the opposing camps were formed. On one side were the benevolent White Magicians, who wished to use the secrets of nature for the benefit of the world at large; and on the other were the Black Magicians, whose purpose was to secure power to fulfill their own desires.

In this conflict, forces so terrific were employed by both parties that at last the very continent was riven and sunk beneath the waters of the ocean; the White Magicians, in their gigantic despair, thus destroying not only themselves but all their world as well, in order to annihilate their enemies of the dark cohorts and to prevent the further dissemination of knowledge which man was not yet fitted to receive. This is to say, they perceived that civilization was a failure with them; that man was better dead than left in possession of knowledge (meaning power) ungenerously employed; that evolution had produced civilization too rapidly upon Atlantis, and must begin the work anew elsewhere.

Such, roughly, was the tradition, as I learned it from curious books years ago,—so many years ago, indeed, that it had passed almost altogether out of my mind when a chance meeting last winter with a French archaeologist in the Djur Djurra Mountains of the Atlas Range recalled and freshened it. This was at Michelet, that surprisingly Alpine appearance among the Algerian clouds where the traveler expects to see Swiss chamois hunters descending the snowy peaks rather than robed and tattooed Arabs, and one must continually doubt that one is in Africa. Professor Paul Lanjuinais, of the Institute, was staying at the inn, and beside the rather inadequate fire in the small smoking room, we fell into talk of the Kabyle people, or "White Arabs," among whom our own party had been motoring. M. Lanjuinais was in the Djur Djurra region for the purpose of research among the Kabyles, he informed us, and presently he mentioned the Atlantean theory of their heavily disputed origin.

"No single theory wholly accounts for the presence of a 'White Arab' here," he said. "Blue-eyed fair people in Africa are spoken of by Egyptian hieroglyphs and rather definitely assigned to this region; my own conclusion is that the Kabyles have been here a very long time. No one can say authoritatively that they may not spring from a flight migration from Atlantis. It is a possible thing, even a rather plausible one; but the same speculation,—for it is a speculation rather than a theory—has been made concerning the Basques, though the language roots of Kabyle dialects and Basque appear to have no relation. However, since if Atlantis existed it was of continental proportion, the peoples upon it were probably of widely different types, even if they were united under a common government." Here M. Lanjuinais paused to laugh. "Occult science, which formerly had an eccentric European prevalence, probably never touched American life, and so you are probably unaware of the occult tales of Atlantis, and do not know that some of the occultists believed themselves to be in possession of the true history of the sinking of the continent. You have never heard anything of that, have you?"

"It happens that I have," I said; and, as he spoke, my memory began to turn the legend up from the obscure stratum of recollections it had come to occupy in my mind. "I think it was this." And I repeated what I recalled of the tradition.

"Yes," he said, laughing again. "That was the substance of the occult vaporizing, if indeed substance may be attributed to what is so extremely tenuous a vapor. I think the occultists put their own rather forced interpretation upon a Berber story someone must have picked up hereabouts years ago and carried either to Europe or to India, perhaps to both."

"Hereabouts?" I asked. "Then there is some trace of a legend of Atlantis among the Kabyle people?"

"Not if one speaks carefully," he replied. "There is a story, yes; but one cannot say that it refers to Atlantis. It speaks of a Great Land to the West in the Waters. That might as well be America, except for the use of the phrase I translated as '*in* the waters', which seems to mean '*within* the waters'."

"You find this story among the Kabyles?"

"Yes. I came upon traces and variations of it here and there; but its best and most complete form appears among them in some of the hilltop villages nearer Bougie, toward the coast."

"How does it differ from the occultist form?"

"In several curious details," M. Lanjuinais replied; and he smiled as a man smiles over something that is between the whimsical and the ridiculous. "Most strikingly of all, it differs in ending with a question that no Kabyle has ever solved and is not to be solved by anyone else, I think."

"But what a strange thing!" I exclaimed. "For a legend to end with a question seems extraordinary."

"But not unique. I believe, however, that there are not many traditions leading to questions as their main point. This one does that. There may be some connection, too, with the fact that the Kabyles do not veil their women; though that is only another speculation, and the story doesn't directly touch upon it."

"What is the story?" I asked. "Would you mind telling us?"

"Not at all," Professor Lanjuinais replied. "It is not too long. In a general way it follows the contour of the occultist legend, especially in representing that governmental control of Atlantis gradually came into the hands of a secret society or sect to which admission was most difficult and involved years of trial, or neophytism. Of course the Kabyles speak of this governing organization as a tribe,—they call it the tribe of Wise People, which may well enough be taken to mean a society of educated persons, initiation taking place upon the completion of education. The Kabyle legend describes them as all-powerful and, until the great dispute arose between the two factions, wholly benevolent. Under their rule, everybody was contented in the whole land. There was no war; public opinion consisted of a general sense of brotherhood; and disease was conquered, for the Wise People could remedy all bodily defects. Also, they could direct the minds and inclinations of the populace, so that there was no such thing as sin. In a word, the 'Great Land in the West' was heaven as a *fait accompli* except for the lack of one item: the people lived to be very old, but they were not immortal. Death was the only fact the Wise People had not conquered; but, save for that, you had a most excellent heaven conducted perfectly by a band of angels, the Wise People; for even heaven itself must be conducted by somebody, one is led to suppose. The invariable circumstance about any organization is that it has officers."

I interposed. "But aren't there some religious organizations?"

"They must have at least a janitor," M. Lanjuinais returned. "And almost always a treasurer. At all events, the Wise People, who of course lived on mountain tops, presumably in fastnesses of learning, ruled this legendary paradise. I think the occultist tradition follows its own purposes in tracing the cause of the dispute to a selfish use of science; but I prefer the Kabyle story, which gives a radically different reason for war."

"The Kabyle version doesn't give the factions as White and Black, benevolent and malevolent?"

"It gives the factions as White and Black," he answered, "but not as benevolent and malevolent. White and Black have no moral symbolic significance in the Kabyle legend; they are simply color designations, as were the Blue and the Gray in your own Civil War. In that war there was a geographical difference between the two parties; in the

White and Black war there was no such line of cleavage; and one of the curious things about it was that every family of the Wise People was divided against itself. In every family there was at least one White member and one Black member, which naturally made the war a bitter one."

"But what caused the war, M. Lanjuinais?"

"I am approaching that," he responded amiably. "Allow me to reach it by degrees. I told you there appeared to be a possible relation between the legend and the fact that the Kabyle women go unveiled; but this I wish merely to suggest and not to emphasize. You have seen these women on the mountain sides, some of them quite handsome in spite of the tattooing upon their faces; and you have observed a few of them in the villages of the valley,—apparent anachronisms among the veiled Mohammedan women. You have caught the glance of these Kabyle girls and women,—a glance a little hard, a little hostile, and, within it, a glint of something wild and driven. A very ancient look, one might call it; a look possibly beset by some historical fear against which there is still rebellion. One might say that a Kabyle woman's eyes are the eyes of a woman who has seen her grandmother beaten to death, but has not been tamed by the spectacle. There is still an antique horror in this glance, and an old, old heritage of defiance. Where did they get such a look? Well, of course one does not need to go back to Atlantis for it; but if one were in a whimsical mood he might trace it to the war between the Whites and the Blacks in the 'Great Land to the West within the Waters.' You see, the curious thing about this war was that all the women were upon one side and all the men upon the other. The women were the Whites and the men were the Blacks."

"Dear me!" I said. "So ancient as that! But what was the point at issue?"

"Whether or not the women should wear veils."

"I see. The women insisted upon casting the veils away, and the men . . ."

"It's not so simple," he interrupted. "In the earlier days, when the Great Land was entirely peaceful, the initiates in knowledge, the Wise People, were all men. At that time the women were merely of the populace, governed benevolently like the rest; but little by little the wives and daughters of the initiates began to steal glimpses of the sacred books and to penetrate the mysteries. In other words, they began to seek education; and of course many of the initiates themselves taught a little magic,—or imparted scientific information,—to their wives and daughters. In those days all the women wore veils; or, as one might express it, they were thoroughly feminine. Gradually, as they acquired more education, and felt more equal to occasions, more able to stand on their own feet, they did not wish to be or seem quite so feminine: some of the bolder among them laid aside their veils and showed their faces openly. Naturally, this caused a little grumbling among the men; but more and more women grew bold, until finally it was thought old-fashioned to wear a veil. Then the women demanded complete initiation into the mysteries of the Wise People. 'We know all about it anyhow,' they said to the men. 'We are your equals in fact, so why deny us the mere acknowledgment of our equality?' There was more grumbling, of course; but the women were initiated, and after that none of them wore a veil. They divested themselves, as it were, of all femininity, and made good their equal footing. Of course some of the men still grumbled: their vanity was not soothed when the women sometimes surpassed them in certain branches of learning and even in special feats of reasoning; but in a general way the men were just, and after a time they accustomed themselves to the new equality. They perceived that it was a necessity if they were to be fair,—although it cannot be said that they ever really liked it,—and within a generation the Wise People consisted of as many women as men. The daughters of the members of the organization were taught as well as the sons, and were initiated with an equal standing. Then, when everything seemed to be settled upon an apparently permanent basis, a strange and unfortunate thing happened. Fashions forever move in cycles; some of the women returned to the fashion of wearing veils. Immediately those who adopted the veil began to be a powerful party within the organization of the Wise People where all were supposed to be equal. They elected all the officers and controlled the organization itself; whereupon seeing their success, all the other women at once resumed the veil and joined them."

I interrupted the narrative of M. Lanjuinais at this point. "Did the men then adopt veils for themselves? Does the Kabyle story mention such a point?"

"No," he replied. "Men are not adapted to veils and are not screened by them. The men among the Wise People could not have helped themselves by wearing veils. But of course they could not endure what the women were doing to them. The men had accepted equality, they could not accept the new inequality; though at first they tried by peaceful means to remedy the disadvantage at which they had been placed. They held a great meeting to discuss the matter. 'You cannot be our equals,' they said to the women, 'and at the same time wear your feminine veils. That is worse than being unfair; it is treachery.'

"But the women laughed. 'When we formerly wore veils,' they said, 'we possessed something that we abandoned when we went unveiled. At the time, we did not perceive our loss, and it has taken us more than a generation to discover it. Now, in again veiling ourselves, we are merely reclaiming our rights,—resuming our natural possession.'

"'No,' the men returned, 'You cannot justly retain this so-called possession of yours, because it is an advantage. Equality means that no one seizes an advantage, and for you to seize this one destroys the equality we have given you and leaves us your inferiors. Our ideal is equality, and to maintain it we will either take the veils away from you or cease to initiate you into the mysteries of our magic and reduce you to your former state of mere usefulness to us.'

"At that the women laughed louder. 'We do not need initiation from you. We possess the mysteries and can do our own initiating. The feminine veil, so alluring and exhaling such charm, is natural to us; it is a part of our long inheritance, and we could not permanently give it up even if we wished to do so, since it is our very instinct

Booth Tarkington

to wear it. If it is your destiny that our attainments and our veiling are to make you our inferiors, you might as well accept it. We accepted our destiny for a long, long time.'

"But the men were unable to be so philosophic as their opponents suggested; in fact, it is related that by this time they were in a condition of the deepest resentment. 'You shall not wear veils,' they said. 'You have abused our sense of justice and insulted our generosity. You shall not wear veils. We have got to know what you are thinking about!'

"Now when the men said they had to take away the veils so they would understand what the women thought, the women raised such a shout of mocking and indignant laughter that the fighting began then and there. Toward morning the survivors withdrew to opposing fastnesses and began their war with sandstorms, which they sent against each other. The Kabyles say the Whites and Blacks used mountain ranges and thunder and lightning as familiar weapons; that they hurled earthquake and tornado upon each other; and that in their last battle they shook the sun so that it rocked in the sky; and the moon, which until then whirled noisily in the heavens like a spinning top, was struck dumb and still, so that it never turned again, and we have only the one face of it always toward us. Then, as the ocean came over the land in waves thousands of feet tall, all the Wise People perished; for the men were determined to the last not to be made inferior by an injustice, and the women, even though they would have made peace at any time, still protested that even if they were willing, they could not give up the veil for it was their very nature itself. That is almost the end of the legend, but not the very end. As I told you, the end is a question; and when the story is told in the evening, in one of the Kabyle huts of stone on a mountain top, the narrator always concludes with the great question. And after that everybody goes to sleep."

"Is there ever any answer to the question?" I asked.

"The Kabyle people think not, and probably they are right. I have suggested that there is an apparent bearing upon it in the fact that the Kabyle women are unveiled and have that ancient driven yet hostile look in their eyes. You see, the tradition implies that the Kabyles escaped from the Great Land. They left at the beginning of the war, before the final cataclysm; but they were only a part of the uninitiated populace of the continent and not members of the Wise People. You perceive how easily it might be misleading to follow such a clue for an answer to the question."

"But what is the question?"

"I suppose of course it was obvious," M. Lanjuinais returned. "'Who won?'"

1926

Joshua Glenn is a consulting semiotician and editor of the websites HiLobrow and Semiovox. The first to describe 1900–1935 as science fiction's "Radium Age," he is editor of the MIT Press's series of reissued proto-sf stories from that period. He is coauthor and co-editor of various books including the family activities guide *UNBORED* (2012), *The Adventurer's Glossary* (2021), and *Lost Objects* (2022). In the 1990s, he published the indie intellectual journal *Hermenaut*.

Algernon Blackwood (1869–1951) is best known as the author of supernatural fiction with cosmic aspirations—including *The Centaur* (1911), *Julius LeVallon* (1916), and *The Bright Messenger* (1921), as well as stories like "The Willows" (1907) and "The Wendigo" (1910). The English author's best-known horror stories, and his series of stories featuring the occult detective John Silence, seek less to frighten than to induce a sense of awe. His work was a significant influence on H. P. Lovecraft and his circle.

Valery Bryusov (1873–1924), a poet, dramatist, art critic, and historian, was one of the principal members of the Russian Symbolist movement. He anticipated giant domed computerized cities, ecological catastrophe, and a totalitarian state in his 1907 story collection *Zemnaya Os (Earth's Axis)*, published in English as *The Republic of the Southern Cross* (1918, translator unknown). Though many of his fellow Symbolists fled the country after the Russian Revolution of 1917, Bryusov remained until his death.

George Allan England (1877–1936) was an American writer and explorer, best known for proto sf-novels including the Darkness and Dawn Series (1912–1914), as well as *The Elixir of Hate* (1910), *The Empire in the Air* (1914), and *The Air Trust* (1915). Like some other proto-sf writers of the era, he was anti-capitalist; in 1912 he ran for Governor of Maine as the Socialist Party of America's candidate. His story "The Thing from—'Outside'" appeared in Hugo Gernsback's magazine *Science and Invention*.

Abraham Merritt (1884–1943), who wrote as A. Merritt, was one of the most successful and influential proto-sf writers of the pulp era. He is best remembered today for his novels *The Moon Pool* (1919), *The Ship of Ishtar* (1924), *The Face in the Abyss* (1931), and *Dwellers in the Mirage* (1932). His stories' suggestion that lost races, ancient technologies, and other far-out phenomena were waiting to be discovered beneath the surface of everyday modern life were a major influence on subsequent sf and fantasy.

Edith Nesbit (1858–1924) was an English author best remembered today for her fantasies for children—written as E. Nesbit, they include *The Wouldbegoods* (1901) and *Five Children and It* (1902)—which have directly influenced everyone from C. S. Lewis and Diana Wynne Jones to J. K. Rowling. In addition to essentially inventing the children's fantasy adventure as we know it, she was author of horror, supernatural, and proto-sf stories. A political activist, she co-founded Britain's socialist Fabian Society.

May Sinclair was the pseudonym of English author and suffragist Mary Amelia St. Clair (1863–1946). She is best remembered for semi-autobiographical novels such as *Life and Death of Harriett Frean* (1922). Sinclair's supernatural and proto-sf tales, which would find champions in T. S. Eliot and Jorge Luis Borges, explore her idiosyncratic take on the idealist notion that reality is a mental construct closely connected to ideas; they were also influenced by contemporary mathematical theories of hyperspace.

Booth Tarkington (1869–1946) was an American author best remembered for *The Magnificent Ambersons* (1918) and *Alice Adams* (1921), both of which won the Pulitzer Prize; as well as for *Penrod* (1914), a collection of comic sketches about the titular 11-year-old boy, and its many sequels. In the 1910s and 1920s he was considered to be America's greatest living author, as important as Mark Twain; today, he is forgotten. An admirer of Charles Fort, Tarkington's only sf story is "The Veiled Feminists of Atlantis."

George C. Wallis (1871–1956) began writing scientific romances in the 1890s. Early stories of interest, besides "The Last Days of Earth," include "The White Queen of Atlantis" (1896), "The Great Sacrifice" (1903), and "In Trackless Space" (1904). His novel *Beyond the Hills of Mist* (serialized 1912) concerns a Tibetan lost race that plans world domination; and his last sf novel, *The Call of Peter Gaskell*, appeared in 1948. He is most likely the only Victorian-era sf writer to continue to publish after World War Two.

H. G. Wells (1866–1946) is best known today as author of pioneering scientific romances such as *The Time Machine* (1895), *The Island of Doctor Moreau* (1896), *The Invisible Man* (1897), and *The War of the Worlds* (1898). An important influence on sf authors from Olaf Stapledon to Arthur C. Clarke, the prodigious English writer was also a social critic and futurist who penned dozens of novels, stories, and works of history and social commentary—in which he proposed more rational ways to organize society.